ENHANCED

TOR BOOKS BY CARRIE JONES

Flying
Enhanced

ENHANCED

CARRIE JONES

TOR TEEN

A TOM DOHERTY ASSOCIATES BOOK
NEW YORK

ENHANCED

Copyright © 2017 by Carrie Jones

A Tor Teen Book
Published by Tom Doherty Associates
175 Fifth Avenue
New York, NY 10010

www.tor-forge.com

Tor® is a registered trademark of Macmillan Publishing Group, LLC.

The Library of Congress Cataloging-in-Publication Data is available upon request.

ISBN 978-0-7653-3658-3 (hardcover)
ISBN 978-1-4668-2850-6 (ebook)

Our books may be purchased in bulk for promotional, educational, or business use. Please contact your local bookseller or the Macmillan Corporate and Premium Sales Department at 1-800-221-7945, extension 5442, or by email at MacmillanSpecialMarkets@macmillan.com.

First Edition: October 2017

Printed in the United States of America

0 9 8 7 6 5 4 3 2 1

To all the people out there who believe.
Thank you. Just believing is an act of power.
Try to hold it close.

Remember upon the conduct of each depends the fate of all.

—Alexander the Great

ENHANCED

Madison Greene hopped up onto a toilet paper holder, shutting the bathroom stall behind her.

This should not be so hard, Madison, she whispered to herself. *This should be easy. Just wait. Just wait for the girl.*

Madison Greene wasn't really her name, but it was the name she had been using. She was a seventh-year infiltrator in the United States, and everything she was sent to do to save the world seemed both difficult and worth it.

At least, it all seemed worth it—except for the probability that she wouldn't survive to see the Earth saved, and she would instead die in a disgusting high school bathroom in southern New Hampshire.

There was no glory in that, was there?

She hauled in a long, slow breath; the Earth air was stale, horrible, and full of chemicals, and it polluted her three lungs. Still, the air did what was required of it to do: kept her breathing and alive.

Another alien was nearby. She could feel him, the violence and death. It was made purely for this: to kill the girl, to kill anything that got in the way of killing the girl. The reasons didn't matter to it. It wasn't about reason. It was just about the death, the purpose.

She couldn't let that happen. She was banking on the girl coming in here after her class. She'd even sent a telepathic suggestion. They would meet. She would give her what she needed to give her. She would warn her. That was Madison's mission.

The transmitter lodged in her hip made sure that whatever happened, the others would know. She shuddered thinking of what could transpire if she failed. All the humans, the silly, amusing humans, would be eradicated, gone before they had a chance to understand what had happened—an entire race destroyed. And yes, humans could be unbelievably stupid—they fought and raped and hated—but they were influenced to do that. Their nature was good. She believed that. She had always believed that. And that's why she wanted to help. Even if it meant dying. She wanted them to survive.

And their best bet was this girl—this untrained, ridiculously confused girl.

The bathroom aromas smelled deadly. The toxic blend of cleaner and old gaseous eruptions was both vile and volatile. The ceiling above her was nonporous and contained the smells of decay. A pipe belched out a noise. She listened. Classes were ending. Footsteps echoed in the halls. The other alien was in the building already. She could hear him breathe. The Formica floor stained with black shoe scuffs and years of use couldn't contain him or her or fate.

The door opened. Madison touched the crystal in her pocket. It was all about this. This rock, which wasn't just a rock, would help the girl find the others. It would help her find her own power. And if Madison survived, she would show her how. And if Madison didn't survive? Hopefully, the girl could figure it out herself.

In the overly bright fluorescent lighting, she could make out the shadow of the girl as she stood by the sinks. The alien was getting closer. She couldn't wait any longer, could she? No. No, if she was going to die here, she was going to make sure the alien died with her, and make sure this girl—this fragile, human girl—survived.

CHAPTER 1

The town has been emptied. When you walk down the street, you meet nobody, nothing, except for the bees buzzing hopelessly in the air, the beetles scuttling across the cracked sidewalks. Nothing seems to matter to the bugs or the wind; they just keep on keeping on. The sky above me is dark, tornado brown and hopeless. The debris the humans left is picked up and spun on.

It's my dream nightmare.

I've had it every night since my mother has been in the hospital. It haunts me in the daytime, too. This dream of a future Earth with no humans, this dream of a future Earth inhabited only by aliens and beetles and bees . . . I can't let it be real.

I am terrified it will be real.

I am terrified that I won't have a chance to stop it.

Human beings like to think that we are the most important species to ever exist, the top of the food chain, the most dangerous predator. There is safety in that. Even as we mourn how awful we are as a species, we can breathe a sigh of relief that though we are awful, we are still safe in that awfulness. Humans don't feel threatened by dolphins. We don't worry that rabbits will attack our phalanx, split our defensive line, capture us, and then roast us on a spit. Our homes aren't threatened by roving bands of manatees bent on our annihilation.

We trust that we are safe. We trust that our biggest threat is each other.

That trust is a lie.

There are much bigger things squelching, stomping, and fluttering about. There are much bigger threats than us humans. Without our weapons, we are a pretty weak species. Our skin breaks and tears. Our minds twist and explode. Our lungs can only bring in so much air. Our muscles can get us to run just barely fast enough—even Olympians can't run fast enough—to escape the threat that approaches us.

And then there is me. There are four facts in the story of Mana Trent.

I am a weapon.

My mother loves me.

My mother is not my biological mother.

My whole life is a lie, a story.

I am a weapon that aliens originally planned to use to infiltrate the humans from within, but I was rescued by my mother, a government-endorsed alien hunter turned rogue, and she created a fabricated life for me before she was kidnapped and shot and spiraled into a coma, which is where she is now—in a coma in a hospital. It is where she has been for weeks and weeks. Now, I'm waiting to be used, to be helpful, for word from the agency she worked for that they need me. So far? Nothing.

The world of desolation, of bees and wind and beetles? It could happen.

This is what I'm thinking about on a freaking freezing day in December. And these thoughts swirl around in my head so fiercely that I forget to answer half the questions on my world history test and instead just doodle all over the margins: WHO AM I? WHAT AM I? WHO DO I TRUST?

My best friend, Seppie, has passed in her test early and sits back at her desk texting or checking out the *cheerleaderswhorock* Tumblr tag or something. Her parents are doctors, normal and brilliant and human. They deal with systemic racism and microaggression with grace and humor, the same way Seppie does. They are the sort of people you want to belong to—smart and funny and perfect in their imperfections.

The bell rings. A dog races outside the classroom window, infinitely more fascinating than the test I should be focusing on. Clouds loom above the dog, thick and gray, heavy with snow that is ready to fall. A front must be coming through, a change in the weather pattern. I shudder.

"Turn your tests in!" our student teacher calls. Her name is Mrs. Horton. We call her Mrs. Horton Hears a Who a lot.

My paper is terribly lacking in answers, kind of like my life. Standing up, I sigh. Seppie nudges me with her bag. "You okay?"

"I feel lost," I tell her.

She pats my arm. Already, Ms. Efficient has packed up her laptop, phone, books, and world history textbook, which weighs eight thousand pounds, while I'm still struggling to get my actual test paper to the teacher's desk.

"I'm sure your mom will wake up soon," she says.

"It's not just that." My head aches.

"Ms. Trent! Kindly stop asking your friend for the answers and turn in your test." Our teacher, Mr. Boland, is not normally quite so much of a pain. He is today.

"I—I—" I can't even get a word out.

And I don't honestly have to speak because while I'm just standing there stuttering and mortified that he thought I might have been cheating, Seppie has whipped my test paper out of my shaking hand and strides to the teacher's desk. She slams it down. Her biceps are definitely looking stronger lately. She has started taking Krav Maga, this Israeli self-defense system designed for the country's special forces.

"I hope you seriously were not implying that Mana was cheating,

Mr. Boland, or that I would help her cheat, because that sort of besmirchment of my character does not suit me nor you." Her hands fly to her hips. "Do I make myself clear?"

He coughs and flattens my paper on the stack of other tests. "Perfectly."

She gives him a glare-down. He looks like a bully that's been beaten up in an alley and I swear if he could turn tail, run, and hide right now, he would. Instead he just pivots to the left, pivots back, his hands go up almost into a V stance, and he adds, "No insult meant."

Everyone remaining in class is silent, standing there, stopped, as we wait for Seppie's reaction.

Finally, she says, "None taken, but you need to apologize to Mana here. She's not the best test taker but she's no cheater. Are you, Mana?"

"No, never," I mumble. I don't mumble because it's a lie. It isn't. It's the truth. I mumble because I'm so horrified.

He laughs nervously. "All set then. Everyone have a lovely day. Try not to be late for class."

As we walk out of the room, Seppie drips disdain. "'Try not to be late for class?' Witness Mr. Needs to Assert His Authority." But as soon as we're out in the hallway and nobody is listening she says, "Sometimes I think you like failing tests."

"Favorite thing in the world," I quip, taking out my phone and checking if there is any communication from China in response to my million texts to him about helping him save the world, or at least humanity. There is nothing.

China is my mother's former partner. He has promised me that I can help him try to locate all these parts in some sort of machine that aliens are making to destroy people. He is arrogant and wears sunglasses a lot and is secretly kind beneath his tough-guy exterior. He is also ignoring my texts.

Seppie yanks the phone out of my hand and scrolls through my unreplied-to texts. She sighs. "How many texts have you sent him?"

"Three a day," I admit. "For a month and a half at least. How long has it been?"

"Fifty-six days." Handing back the phone, she cocks her head toward me, chin down. This is Seppie's sad posture. It's the same way she looked when we lost the cheerleading state championship in eighth grade because Doreen Dwyer forgot to do a back handspring and then later fell out of a simple prep and elevator. We lost by a point. Seppie never forgave her. And then there was the time Seppie did not get a perfect 2400 on her SATs and got a 2390 instead. I couldn't talk to her for a week. Nobody could. Lyle and I eventually sat her down for an intervention that involved binge-watching *Scream Queens* and lots of chocolate ice cream.

I feel like I would get a full-on Seppie lecture about seeming desperate in texts and how you should never act too needy, except that she has class now and we've come to the intersection in the hallway where we always part.

She gives me a tiny hug. "Listen. Some things are just not meant to be. Maybe it just isn't your destiny to save the world. It's okay. You're okay."

Her words sting. I stiffen even though I'm being hugged. "I don't have any other destiny. I'm supposed to be helping them."

"Sweetie, if they wanted your help, I think they would have texted you back by now." Her words stay in the air for a second and thud to the floor, hard and heavy things. She lets go of me, hug over.

"I know you think I can't help—"

"This is an alien versus humanity thing, Mana. This is war." Seppie's voice is low but insistent.

"I know it's a war."

"Why do you have to be a part of it? There's no reason you have to go through all that again. Your mom is in the hospital."

"I know that."

"Your dad is missing."

"I know that!" I talk over her. "That's why I have to do something. Don't you get it?"

"No. I don't. You can stay here, right here, and be safe."

"There is no safe. Come on, Seppie. You know that now. There are people like my mom and China laying down their lives for us— these . . . these silent heroes—and I have to be a part of that. I can't not be a part of that. I can't do any less than that. You've seen what I can do."

I want to keep arguing, but her words hurt and I say nothing else as her face shifts from sympathetic Seppie to an expression that I've never seen before.

"I—um—I got into a special camp," she says out of nowhere. "It's sort of a premed, precollege thing for people who want to be doctors."

She's leaving me? Now?

The floor is suddenly super-attractive and I want to stare at it, but instead I manage to rally and throw myself into Seppie in a congratulatory hug. "Really? I am so happy for you! When? Where?"

"Soon. I—um—I'm probably going to miss some school." She hugs me back and whispers into my hair, "You sure it's okay? I feel weird leaving you."

This seems sudden and for a second I don't trust her, which is ridiculous. I mean, I *trust* my friends, but I keep expecting her to shake her head and make the sign of the cross and tell me she's not up for all the weirdness and danger that are my life now. She hasn't, though. I have to give her that.

I give her an extratight squeeze and try to talk through the lump of sadness that has lodged itself in my throat. "Of course! I'm a big girl. I can handle myself without my best friend for a week or so. Right?"

She breaks the hug, but keeps her long arm wrapped over my shoulder. "Of course you can. You can do anything, Mana. You just have to put your mind to it."

"Thanks, life coach," I quip.

"Best friends are often life coaches."

"Sure, if their advice is 'go kiss that cute guy over there,' or 'yes, climb out the window so we can sneak into some twenty-one-and-over club.'" Laughing makes it better, but the reality sets in again. "How long will you be gone?"

"A week or two. The details are still being worked out." She cringes. "I won't be here to cheer for a bit, but I'll be back in time for Districts."

I try to process it all, but it just makes me sadder. "Wait. When do you leave?"

"Tomorrow."

"Tomorrow?"

"It's been very last minute, rush-rush," she says, but her voice doesn't ring 100 percent true. "It'll be fine. Don't worry."

She folds me into another quick hug and lets go. She doesn't scrutinize my face because she knows me well enough to predict that I won't be able to hide my sadness. Neither of us wants that.

"Try to have all your life crises internally when I'm gone, okay? All your big questions? Just stand by on figuring them out, and try not to have any big external emergencies! You know what I mean, right?" she shouts over her shoulder as she disappears into the classroom.

And the crap thing about it is not just that I have failed my world history test, but that the answers to those questions that were spiraling around in my head throughout the exam suck. *Who am I?* I will never know. *What am I?* Some sort of experimented-on freak. *Who do I trust?*

It has been weeks and we haven't looked for anything at all.

So, yeah, these were the things that I was thinking about instead of answering why governments in the Middle East back in ancient times weren't centralized or why pre-Columbian civilizations were similar to classical Greece. Clue: It's all about the city-states, which I knew, but I was too distracted to answer.

I barely held it together when I stared at those blank spaces. And then Mr. Boland was such an ass, accusing me of cheating.

"Mana?" Mrs. Horton is notoriously wine-loving, which you can tell from the red veins in her eyes, but she is also notoriously kind, and I know she can tell that I'm upset, thanks to the blank piece of paper Seppie turned in for me and my currently shaking hands. She comes around from the other side of the hall. "Are you doing okay?"

I nod stiffly. I don't trust my voice. I'm not good when people are kind to me or when they ask about my mother.

"How is your mother doing?" she asks, right on cue.

I freeze. There are kids behind me. I will not lose it. I drop my bag. Stuff falls out all over the floor.

"She's the same," I lie. She *is* the same physically—still in a coma—but she is not the mother, the quiet, demure, non-alien-hunting mother, that I thought she was for all the years of my growing up. "I'm sorry about the test."

I squat to pick up my things and Mrs. Horton helps.

Her face squishes up a bit as she studies my face and then her attention focuses on the other students streaming past me down the hallway. She hands me my world history book. "We can talk about this later."

My F.

We can talk about my F is what she means.

"Okay," I say and scurry off. Now that my pen and stuff are back in my bag, I escape down the hallway without making eye contact with anyone and head toward lunch, but I completely do not want to go to lunch. I want to cry, because seriously? Seppie leaving after I've failed my world history exam is the final straw in the Mana Entrance to Nervous Breakdown Land. I don't want to whine, but I'm already dealing with a lot of world-changing crap, which includes trying to keep the entire human race from dying without my actually doing anything. It seems ironic that the class I'd be failing would be world history. Soon, there may be no humans left who will care about world history.

I start texting China—just one more time.

"Mana!" Seppie's voice calls after me and she runs down the now empty hallway. I'm not sure why she's left class and whatever she was going to say is forgotten once she sees my phone in my hand. "Are you really texting him again?" She takes a step back, exhaling, probably remembering how I stopped bullets midflight, knocked men and women down simply by the crazy anger that happened in my mind after I had some caffeinated Coke. "It is not up to you to save the world, Mana. You have nothing to prove."

The bell rings.

"It's not about me."

She taps my phone with her perfect fingernail. "Stop texting. It makes you seem desperate."

She pivots away even as I yell after her, "But I *am* desperate."

The hallways are empty. And I need to go somewhere or else I'll get a detention for loitering.

So, I bomb into the bathroom in the foreign-language wing. This is the bathroom nobody ever uses because it smells like dead mice and Clorox bleach wipes all at once. I smash open a stall with my fist, all macho and stuff, ready to hunker down on the toilet and cry in an un-macho way . . . but there she is, standing on top of the toilet paper holder, ruining my plans.

"What—?" I start to speak but my words sort of strangle in my throat. I've never seen this girl before. She balances on that tiny perch with just one bare foot. Her toes, not her toenails, are yellow. They match her hair.

She puts her finger to her normal-colored lips. She appears human, but she's not—even I can tell that. "Shh . . ."

"What?" I point at my chest. "Me?"

Her head bobs this way and that. She cocks it to the side like a dog does, listening. "Shh . . ."

"But what? Why am I shh-ing?"

Reaching out, she yanks me into the stall, hauling me up in the air in a swift, easy movement. I dangle there. She uses her free foot to slowly nudge the stall door shut. Yep. Definitely not human.

"You might want to lock it . . . the door, I mean," I whisper when I remember how to talk again.

Her eyes widen and she says in a deep croak, "Good idea."

With a quick release and grab, she shifts her point of contact with me to the back of my sweater, which panics me slightly because I don't want it to rip. My mom is in the hospital, my dad is missing, and I'm a bit low on funds so I can't ruin all my clothes unless I want to suddenly pretend to be Goodwill chic. I'm not quite ready for that commitment yet. Even as she pulls the catch-and-release-and-catch maneuver, the alien girl pushes the latch of the door shut with her big, yellow toe. Peppermint swirls suddenly appear on her yellow toenails, which is absolutely amazing, and I would love to find out who did that because I am in dire need of cool toenails.

"Your nails," I whisper, "are adorable."

She actually smiles. Her teeth are normal like a human's. Just then the door to the bathroom creaks opens and her grin disappears into a determined line. She puts her finger to her lips, but she doesn't have to tell me. I know enough to be quiet.

The whole feel of the bathroom changes. Tension fills the air. Whatever has just stepped in here with us is most certainly not human.

All the alien girl's muscles quiver as if in anticipation of a fight. Her nostrils twitch. The stall door, marred with beautiful graffiti illustrating in black ink a bum having an explosive poop, keeps us from seeing who or what just came into the bathroom with us. I check above the compartment's walls. There's no drop ceiling to escape through. We can hardly dive through the toilet and into the pipes. We are stuck in the tiny space, stuck, waiting. Fear pushes my heart into overdrive.

Something is with us.

Don't check in here. Don't check in here. The words flop around inside my head like a prayer. *Don't check in here. Don't check . . .*

No sound fills the bathroom. This is obviously weird all by itself. People don't come in the bathroom and just stand there doing nothing. They wash their hands or use the toilet or open their purse and get stuff out to brush their hair or smoke something illegal or pop pills or gossip, but they never, ever just come in the bathroom and make no sound.

The alien girl tenses.

I tense, too.

I'm afraid to breathe.

I can't believe I'm even trusting my life and safety to an alien girl I haven't met before. However, she *does* have nice toenails. Lyle says I am too trusting. Lyle is my other best friend besides Seppie, and we kissed once and it was beautiful, but now we're both dealing with identity issues since he's turned out to be an alien and we're also dealing with absent mothers. Mine is hospitalized. His is jailed. Still, he's probably eating in the cafeteria right now, safe and full. My brain is babbling.

Something is with us, something bad.

The girl gives me *Be quiet!* eyes, even though I didn't say anything. A spider crawls across the top of the bathroom stall door. Two seconds later a giant tongue curls up around it and then disappears, trapping the spider and sucking it away. The world smells of moldy bread and death. Fear gags me.

Maybe, I think, *it won't notice we're here.*

Maybe, I think, *we should run.*

In the next second, everything goes straight to hell.

The stall door slams open. The lock turns out to be a flimsy, useless thing against the force of the creature on the door's other side.

Standing there, it appraises us for half a second.

It's monstrous, large, and green, like you imagine orcs or trolls from fairy tale books. Only there are four eyes on its head instead of two, and its head is long and pointy and strangely undersize on top of its enormously muscled shoulders.

I study it, looking for a weakness, a something, a way to escape. Instead I freeze.

It is naked.

So grossly naked.

But I can't tell if it's male or female. Or both?

"How did it even get in here?" I yell. I scream a swear word. Luckily, the walls in this part of the building are five thousand years old (not really) and thick. I don't think anyone can hear anything coming from a bathroom or another classroom, ever. I hope not, at least. I don't want anyone else coming in here and getting hurt. I swear again.

The alien girl matches my curse and jumps straight up into the air, hauling me with her and then moving sideways a couple feet. "Tuck your legs!"

I do and we vault to the next stall, where she lands perfectly on another toilet paper holder. There's no time to say anything or even breathe, because the monster thing moves to that stall, too. Its tongue flicks out toward us.

"Again!" she yells and jumps back to our original stall, even as she yells the word.

It may be big, but it isn't stupid, and it's right there behind us.

I smash-kick the door at the thing's face. The door hits its nose, but bounces right back open. Alien girl lets out some impossible groan and the monster's tongue lashes out again. We move up and over. This time she lands in the toilet. Her naked foot falls into the bowl, which is disgusting and horrible. A hard cracking noise fills the stall. She drops me and cries out. I try to yank her up.

She shakes her head. "It's broken."

Broken. Her foot? The toilet? It doesn't matter. What matters is surviving.

"How do we fight it?" I ask. "How?"

Before she can answer, there it is again at the door. It towers over us, a hulking, naked form.

I have no weapons, just my Hello Kitty backpack, but there are books in it. I rip it open and yank out my world history book. I throw it as hard as I can at the creature's face. It makes impact. The thing grunts and lashes its tongue out toward me. The alien girl lunges sideways, her foot still stuck in the toilet. The tongue wraps around her waist. The force is enough to free her from the toilet, but it also makes a sickening noise like all her internal organs have been crushed and flattened.

"Run!" Her eyes bulge as the creature yanks her closer to its mouth. "You idiot! Run, Mana!"

She knows my name. She also knows I am a bit of an idiot.

"Mana! Go!"

She tried to protect me from this . . . this thing . . . And of course, everyone has been ignoring me and yet, here I am, fighting aliens in the grossest bathroom at school, and none of my friends are backing me up. Just the poor alien girl.

There's no way in hell I'm going to leave her here and run away. Anger makes my head vibrate. Yanking the toilet seat off the toilet, I try not to think about germs and bacteria from poop and vomit and stuff, and instead rush forward right at the creature. Its mouth seems toothless but full of sucker-like things. I smash the toilet seat into it, just above the tongue, pushing as hard as I can. The creature's arm smacks me backward and I'm airborne before my side slams into the wall by the sinks. It takes me a second, but only a second, before adrenaline and pure rage have me rushing forward again.

"Don't hurt her!" I yell.

The ugly alien starts sputtering and coughing, and the alien girl is not in its mouth, which is good. I grab the world history book and jump up to smoosh it into the thing's mouth, too, just above the toilet seat, which thankfully is still lodged in there.

"Eat history, butt head." I mutter this like I'm some kind of badass myself, but I'm shaking, not a badass; not just angry, but terrified.

His tongue tries to get back into his mouth.

I have given it a gender affiliation.

I rip open the garbage bin and shove the rounded, metal top into his mouth, too.

"Girl! Are you okay?" I shout.

There's a grunt from somewhere, but I can't focus on that now, can't take my attention off the alien.

The eyes turn to examine me and then they pulsate and bulge, pupils widening and twitching before all four of them roll into his head. He falls, grabbing on to me. We tumble down to the tiled floor, hitting hard. Pain billows through my arm, my knee, but it's not a forever-pain, more like I've landed in a bad back twist and wrenched a muscle.

Two seconds later, I have scrambled out from beneath the wretched thing's arm and I'm trying to find the alien girl. She's on the other side of his gasping, twitching body. I have to clamber over him to reach her. She's an odd bluish-yellow color, even for an alien. I unwrap the tongue from the center of her torso, ignoring its sliminess, and lift up her shirt a bit to inspect the damage.

Everywhere the tongue touched, her skin has turned blackish purple. I must gasp or something, because she shakes her head. The alien beast from Shrek Gone Wrong Land has stopped moving.

"You have taken its life journey," she whispers, "and it has taken my life journey from me."

I start to protest but she grimaces and reaches into the pocket of her pants. "I was bringing this to you. That is why . . . I'm here. And to warn you. They are trying to kill you and all like you. The Samyaza. They know you are here now. He is proof . . ."

Her voice pauses and stops. It is a hoarse whisper, a last vocalization. My heart breaks for her and when she reaches her hand out to me, it trembles.

"Take it," she insists. "Please."

I grab a black crystal from her hand. It looks like it's made up of chunks of tiny rectangles all latched together somehow, and it shines and reflects light like police officers' sunglasses in old movies. The stone pushes against my skin like it wants to hide in my palm, to just run away from the death, the bathroom, the world. It feels . . . happy, safe, good. I wrap my fingers around it. It just fits.

"Don't let anyone see it. Don't let anyone have it. Don't tell anyone. It will help you locate the others. You must keep it safe. She trusts you—" She loses her ability to talk for a second and her eyes close. "She wants you to—"

"No . . . hey . . . Stay here . . . I need to thank you. I need you to be okay . . . And . . . open your eyes," I beg her, forgetting about the crystal the moment I place it on the floor next to her.

There is still movement beneath the lids. That has to be a good sign.

"We have to get you help," I say. I grab her hands in mine. They are blackening even as I hold them. The color spreads like spilled watercolor paint, taking over her skin. "I can call China, maybe? They must have a way to help you."

"No. You can't tell anyone. Not even him."

"You aren't with them? Isn't that why you're here? To activate me? Make me an agent?"

"You aren't some weapon to be activated, Mana. Remember that. You are a living being. A soul. With choices." Bluish liquid drips out of her mouth and she convulses. Once. Twice. Her eyes open and lack lucidity, but then they refocus, right on me. "Your destiny is not to be used by others. That is a big lie. It is a lie you can choose, but not a lie that you might want . . ." A gurgle obscures her words. She keeps talking through it and I've lost what the lie is. ". . . and Pierce says you can be trusted. She says you are kind."

Pierce! Pierce was the alien who worked with my mom and China. We thought she died. Nobody has talked to her since we left her defending a compound against some aliens.

"Is Pierce alive? Is she okay? Is she with China?"

The alien starts to answer but instead of words, another gurgling noise comes out of her mouth. "No more talking!" I wipe at her face with some paper towels that are on the floor. "We have to get you help. Now. No arguing."

"My organs are crushed," she says. "It is not your fault. I should have been better—faster. That toilet . . . So sorry . . ."

"You were great. You jumped over the stalls and you had the best balance, and your toenails—" The words burble out even as my stomach twists with worry and sorrow. There's no way that I can save her.

"You are a sweet girl, Mana. Please, take the crystal. Don't let anyone know. They will want it. Use it to find the rest. The link. They are there."

"The rest of what?"

Her eyes open. "It will help you find other enh—"

And then she is gone. Her words stop. Her breath stops. Her eyes don't move. Her hands in mine are heavy weights.

"Don't go," I whisper. "Please, I like you. And you know things. Please . . . Don't go."

But there is no point in begging, because she is already gone.

CHAPTER 2

The shock begins with hints of silence first, with little nuggets of fear and repulsion. Two dead aliens rest on the floor in front of me—the floor of the foreign-language-wing bathroom, the floor of the room that already smells of dead mice and stagnation and bleach. At last, I manage to breathe again, to move. I am no heroine; this is obvious as I stare down at the bodies. A heroine would have saved the alien girl who was trying to save her. A heroine would not have just barely managed to kill the bad guy with a toilet seat. There would be no good-guy deaths if I were a heroine. I would be perfect and beautiful and not gasping for breath in this horrible place.

Why were they both here? Why do I have a crystal? Why did she die for me? And who is trying to kill me? And what did she mean about me not just being a weapon, that my destiny is my own choice? Were those just some dying thoughts, a lesson on the age-old debate between determinism versus free will? And then there's the whole thing about using the crystal to find something. What kind of something? Other pieces of the machine that's supposed to destroy humanity? Or all of alien life? Or something?

And if I can use the crystal to find bits of the machine, couldn't she, too? Isn't that what we were originally going to try to use the chip that my mother had for? If that's even what she was trying to say . . .

The crystal suddenly revolts me.

I don't want to do this all over again, I suddenly realize. I don't want to kill people. I don't want to be confused and protecting some random object that I don't understand.

A noise like gas being expelled fills the room. Even in death, the orc thing is obnoxious. Its tongue swells.

The girl's toenails are so sad now. The peppermint swirls don't remind me of candy canes any longer. Instead, they are the eddying abyss of loss.

She brought this crystal to me for a reason. She died for that reason.

"Don't trust her," I mutter out loud. "You can't trust anyone."

But if someone dies for you, doesn't that mean you *can* trust them? She said not to call China for help. So she wasn't aligned with China. But she did mention Pierce who was aligned with China. Who was she aligned with, then? It's so confusing.

I call China.

There is no answer.

We like to think of things in terms of sides, like teams you cheer for. There is the light and there is the dark. There are the good guys and there are the bad guys. It's why sports are so popular. The game you watch is a story that has a beginning, a middle (halftime), and an end. You have a side you want to win. You have a side that you want to lose. You have the final score, which is nice closure. But real life, unfortunately, isn't like that. There is no nice set beginning, middle, and end, not just two teams to be on, and sometimes there is no winner or loser. It sucks that it isn't so simple and easy, because I want simple and easy right now. I want to know where to align myself, or even to just know who the freaking teams are.

My thoughts jumble and circle around each other, like a snake eating its own tail, tangled up in itself. I don't know what to do with the dead aliens. It seems disrespectful to just go. I can't report this to the principal. I can't just leave them here. I am traumatized into inaction, which is not what it is to be a heroine. Heroines act.

But here I am, listening to the water in the pipes and the silence, expecting there to be some lesson to be learned in all of this quick and instant terrifying nothingness.

And for what?

So that I could be kept alive.

And for the crystal in my pocket.

She wanted to give it to me. She trusted me. She knew what I am supposed to do, what I have been modified to do.

Reaching down with my trembling hand, I close her eyelids to hide the blankness of her eyes and whisper, "Thank you."

I kick the giant tongue out of the way. I don't want it near her.

"I'm so sorry," I tell her, and then I take off out of the windowless bathroom to find Lyle. There's no way I'll be strong enough to move that big-ass, ugly alien guy by myself. And I want to move him, get away, get out of here, see the cloudy sky above me, even breathe in the cold air.

But I pause. I go back inside, get my backpack, zip it up again. The history book is a goner, but that's not the end of the world. Ripping out a piece of paper, I scrawl the words *BATHROOM IS CLOSED* across it and stick it on the door with some gum. Pretty disgusting, but it's the best I can do. I don't want random innocents wandering in here.

*E*very one of my footsteps echoes through the empty hallways, like some sort of battle call or other attention-seeking sound. I try to be quiet, try not to run, but it takes everything I have to control myself. Someone could walk into the bathroom and see the aliens. Someone's entire reality could shatter unless I hurry and get Lyle, and get back and move the bodies before they are discovered. And where will we move them? I wonder as I patter down the stairs to the main floor where the cafeteria is. How do you hide bodies?

I open the doors to the cafeteria and scan the tables for Lyle's messy hair. Luckily, he's tall and I spot his floppy-haired head at a table of jocks before my panic becomes all-consuming. I stride over there. They are discussing this graphic novel about Alexander the Great. It has a lot of sex scenes in it.

Lyle is saying with his mouth full, "It's historically accurate. The sexuality is not a big deal. Plus, there's gold in the book. It's amazing."

I touch his shoulder. "Um . . . Lyle . . ."

He's munching on a piece of cheese pizza that's absolutely covered with grease and he looks up at me. So do the rest of the guys. "Yeah?"

I clear my throat, totally awkward. "Can you come with me for a second?"

Some of the guys start making heckling noises.

"I'm kind of eating my pizza. Can you give me a sec?" He says this in a nicer way than the words themselves sound.

"Um . . . yeah . . . no." I grab him by the arm and yank him away from the table, which only increases the heckling.

Keegan McKim says, "Oh. . . . Uh-oh . . . Lylie's in troub-ble."

Keegan McKim may be salutatorian but the boy is not original. Grayson Staggs snatches Lyle's pizza out of his hand and immediately starts eating it himself.

Lyle, thankfully, doesn't even get cranky. He just follows me out of the cafeteria, keeping pace with my fast and furious walk.

"What is it?" he asks as I shove open the glass doors. "Wait. Is it your mom? Is your mom okay?" He runs a hand through his hair and hugs me before I can answer. For a second, in his arms, I feel a little safer, a little better, and then he says, "Crap. I'm so sorry, I didn't think. I was really into that pizza. Crap. I suck. She didn't d—?"

Against my better judgment, I pull away from his hug and interrupt. "No. That's not it . . . She's the same."

"Whew." He studies me. "But it's important, right? Because . . . pizza."

I should have gone and got Seppie even if she is in class. Lyle,

I think, was a horrible choice for a helper. No offense to Lyle. But then his face shifts into something more smiling and I realize he was teasing. He yanks me into a hug and I whisper, "Jerk."

And he says back, "Jerk."

He pats my back three times in a pretty bro way and we part, smiling at each other, before I remember that this is urgent and important.

"So," he says, before I begin, "is this something dangerous or something school related?"

"Both." I grab him by the shoulder and start walking with him down the hallway despite the fact that we have no hall pass. "There is a dead alien in the foreign-languages bathroom in the A wing."

He stops walking. "What?"

"I said that there is a dead alien girl in the foreign-languages bathroom in the A wing. Plus, a sort of dead monster-alien-orc thing with this crazy gross tongue."

"Whoa. You went in that bathroom? Everyone knows it smells in there."

"Tangent, Lyle. Tangent." I groan.

Lyle and I both tend to digress. Seppie can't stand it.

"Okay, okay. Sort of dead? Or sort of monster? Which do you mean?" Lyle asks.

"Dead. Monster. Alien. I don't know why I said sort of. Sorry. I'm stressed."

"No worries. I'm trying to add some levity, so you don't panic. So, there's a dead alien girl and a dead alien monster." He has super-long legs and when he starts hurrying, I have to pretty much jog to keep up. "In the bathroom. Why?"

"There was this, um . . . weird alien fight?"

"And you were just randomly there?"

"Sort of. I mean, I was, but the dead alien girl was waiting for me. She wasn't dead yet, obviously. Yeah. Maybe not obviously?" My voice is creeping up into high notes, which is what happens when I get slightly hysterical. I lower it as we climb the staircase and give him a brief outline of what happened.

He stops right outside the bathroom. "She gave you what?"

I pull the crystal out of my pocket, unfold my hand, and show him. "Crap."

"Why crap?"

"Because it's got to be important. She sought you out, gave it to you, and now she's dead. That's why."

My lips sort of turn in to my mouth. My hand holding the crystal trembles. Lyle uses his own fingers to curl mine closed around it. "You should probably put that in your pocket or something and keep it safe."

"Yeah."

"Yeah."

I do exactly that, stuffing it into the front pocket of my jeans, which are getting too loose because when I am stressed I lose weight. The crystal is a lump there, heavy and solid, bulging out of my jeans, a reminder of what has just happened. Lyle watches me do this and then reaches out toward the door. I grab his arm, preventing him from opening it.

"What?" His voice isn't annoyed, more worried.

"I don't know. I'm just stressed. I'm not a big alien expert. What if the bad one comes back to life or something?"

"You choked it with a toilet seat, Mana." He shakes his head. "Unbelievable."

"And my world history book helped." I punch his arm. "I know it's absurd."

"It's amazing."

"There are dead things in there, Lyle. Some nice alien girl with pretty toenails died for me."

He holds up his hands. "I know! I know, I'm sorry, but you're the only person I know who would kill something with a toilet seat."

"Shut up, Lyle."

"Okay. Okay. Sorry."

He reaches out to open the door one more time, and then jumps back.

A horrible little scream leaps out of my throat. "What? Is it hot? Did it burn you? Did you hear something?"

"No . . . It's just . . . It's the girls' bathroom. Do you know how much trouble I'll get into if I get caught going in the girls' bathroom?" His eyes are big and terrified.

"Seriously, Lyle?"

"Seriously."

"Lyle. When we first met China, you were in the girls' locker room. It was the same thing."

"No. That time Deputy Bagley was with me, so it wasn't like I was just this random skeevy guy in the girls' locker room."

"Lyle!"

"What?"

"This is ridiculous."

With a brisk movement of his head, he says, "You're right. You're right, sorry! Going in now. Heading right in. Yep. Here we go." He checks the empty hallway like he expects a teacher or our principal to magically appear. "Yep. Going in."

"Lyle! Man up." I shove him a tiny bit and he rushes into the bathroom. I'm right behind him.

He stops dead still in the center of the room. Now he's annoyed. I can tell by how his shoulders aren't square.

"Mana? Not funny." His hands go to his hips. "I know you're bored. I know you want to do something epic, and you're tired of waiting for China, but you can't start making things up."

"I'm not."

"Look around you."

The bathroom is empty. There is no Shrek-like alien guy with a massively long tongue. There is no alien girl with peppermint-swirl toenails.

"Someone took the bodies." I sigh out the words.

"That quick? How long were you gone?"

"Ten minutes tops." I think about it some more and start opening up the stalls like the bodies could possibly be hidden in there. One after the other, they are empty. "It was really more like five. And my sign's gone. I put a sign on the bathroom door."

"Mana . . ." Lyle has crossed his arms over his chest.

"Lyle, I swear to you that I am not making this up!"

He eyes me. "Mana . . . I know you're under a lot of pressure right now. I know that maybe you're trying to take the focus off your world history test and your mom and my mom and . . . and maybe, you know . . ."

"I. Am. Not. Lying. Lyle." I whirl on him and give him a full glare. "And that is the worst thing you could ever say to me."

He backs up a step, bumping his butt on the sink. "I'm not saying lying on purpose, necessarily, but even the strongest people crack under this sort of pressure."

"Lyle . . . I would not make up an alien that would resemble Shrek."

"You've always liked Shrek."

"Exactly! So I would not make him a bad guy." I sniff around. "And smell. Doesn't it smell different in here?"

"It smells like dead mice."

"And what else?"

"Bleach."

"What else?"

"Um. . . ." He sniffs. He makes a big production of inhaling. He sniffs again. "Copper?"

"Copper! Like blood!"

"Was there blood?"

"No. But it smells like it."

"No, it smells like copper."

"Copper smells like blood!" I insist.

"It does?"

"Yes."

We stand there for a moment. Neither of us says anything. Lyle runs a hand through his moppy hair. This is the second time he's done that in the last few minutes, which means he's stressed and trying to hide it. For a second, I feel sort of bad. He didn't choose this any more than I did. It's not easy finding out you aren't human (him), or that you're an enhanced human (me).

"How about the toilet seat," he finally asks. "Didn't you say you suffocated him or something with a toilet seat?"

"Brilliant!" I leap forward, grab his face with my hands, and kiss his nose. He instantly blushes, but I'm too psyched to bask in the reddening of his face. Instead, I pivot and rush into the stall. "Crap."

He stifles a laugh. "Appropriate word there, Mana." He's right behind me, staring at the toilet seat, which is in its proper place atop the toilet.

"I can't believe this," I say, bending over and checking it out. "It's like they have conjured up the—"

A voice, loud and adult, comes from behind Lyle. "Excuse me. Stop whatever you are doing."

Lyle makes a tiny shriek noise and whirls around. I grab at the toilet seat and whirl around, too. The toilet seat pops up into my hands. It wasn't bolted down.

Our principal, Mrs. Sweet, stands in the doorway, hands on her hips, lips pursed, looking down her short nose at us.

"Lyle Stephenson. What exactly are you doing in the girls' bathroom? Don't answer that. I see Ms. Trent is here with you. This is not the place for a romantic rendezvous."

Lyle freezes in a good-boy panic. Lyle never, ever gets in trouble. I am not going to let that start now.

"He was taking care of me," I babble. One of my hands holds the toilet seat. The other wipes at my mouth. Then I realize that hand had also been clutching the toilet seat a second ago. This germy reality panics me more than Mrs. Sweet does.

Mrs. Sweet raises an eyebrow. "And how was he doing that?"

"I threw up," I say, making my voice a little more trembly and a lot more embarrassed. "I don't know if I'm *sick* sick or if it's because I bombed my world history test, but I knew I was going to throw up and I'm afraid of throwing up. I mean, I'm totally phobic about it, and Lyle knows that, and I was panicking and he was just being . . . He was just being nice."

She takes a step away from me, which means she is now holding the door open with her hip. The hallway is empty beyond her. "Do you still feel like you are going to vomit?"

I nod. "A little."

Lyle makes a tiny moan noise.

"You are aware that you broke the toilet seat?" she asks.

I nod again. "I . . . I . . . I'm sorry."

Extending my arm, I offer the toilet seat to her. She makes an incredibly distasteful face, which involves the squinching up of her nose and flattening of her lips. For a second, I almost think that she is an alien.

"You two . . . You both . . ." She actually sputters. "I will be keeping an eye on you. I expected more from you, Mr. Stephenson. However, I have often observed how a fine, upstanding young gentleman's behavior can be maligned by the subpar company he keeps."

We stand there. She stares at us. I stare at her. Mrs. Sweet just insulted me.

"Are you saying . . . ?" Lyle cocks his head. "Mana isn't subpar."

My heart soars a bit.

The bell rings. "If you aren't feeling well, Mana, you should go home. You don't want to spread contagion in the school." She wrinkles her nose like I'm the contagion.

"Okay. Yeah." I *will* go home.

"Lyle, you should go to class." She leaves us, pivoting without another word. The bathroom door slams shut behind her. Lyle and I stand in the death-smelling bathroom and for a moment we are actually silent. His breath leaves his mouth in one big relieved whoosh.

"She said 'keeping an eye on you.' That's disgusting. It's like you pluck your eye out and put it on someone's shoulder or something," I say, replacing the toilet seat and hustling over to the sinks to wash my hands. "Thank you for defending me."

"Mana. We almost got in trouble." Lyle's voice is monotone. Which is so unlike him. Poor Lyle.

"It's okay. We didn't."

"I know . . . I know, but . . . I don't know if I can do this anymore."

I start pacing back and forth in front of the sinks. Subpar. I'll show her subpar. "Do what?"

"This." He gestures wildly around. "Whatever 'this' is."

"Us? Do you mean us? Or do you mean the dealing-with-aliens thing?"

In the silence that follows, my heart sort of cleaves. I get what he's saying. I just don't want to get what he's saying.

Finally, he whispers, "I don't know? Both?"

Both?

"But you—you've always wanted adventure. You've always wanted aliens. You have a TARDIS mug from *Doctor Who*. There is a life-size Spock cutout in your bedroom. You . . . you are the most curious person I know, Lyle. You can't mean this. What do you mean? You aren't making sense."

"I . . ." He looks around. His eyes redden a bit, matching his skin, which is still flushed from blushing before. "I . . . I don't know. I just don't know if I can handle this."

"Handle what? Aliens? Or me?" Hurt sizzles inside my chest.

He swallows so hard that I can actually hear it. "I love you, Mana. You know I love you, but I'm not . . . My mom always said that—"

"Your mother? Your mother! You are dumping me because of your mother?"

"I didn't say I was dumping you." He pauses. "Are we even going out? Officially?"

"Whatever. You said you didn't know if you could quote-unquote *handle us*. That sounds a lot like dumping to me."

His mouth moves but no sound comes out.

"I can't believe you," I whisper. "I can't believe you could do this. We've been friends forever. You're better than this, Lyle. You are stronger than this."

"But I'm not. That's the thing. I'm not." He bites his lip. I have seen him bite his lip multiple times in my life but every single time was when he was lying to his mother.

I can't handle this. Not now. I turn coward and rush out of the bathroom of death and into the hall. The bell rings and doors fly open, but the bathroom door slams closed, shutting Lyle out of my life. I join the people heading to classes and lunch and important destinations and pretend like I'm one of them—a person who knows where she is going—but I'm not. I'm really, really not.

Lyle has dumped me. Lyle has fizzled out. The guy who has been one of my best friends forever. The guy who had a *Doctor Who* fixation before it was almost sort of cool. The guy who has believed in aliens since he was, like, four years old. And back then he didn't know he was one. The guy who wanted to be a Jedi knight and save the universe. This guy . . . this guy has dumped me in a friendship way.

He said he wasn't dumping you, I tell myself, but that's just semantics. He said that he couldn't handle this—the alien thing. This same guy jumped into a truck and helped me kill a Wendigo and now he can't handle it. He's an alien. What does he even mean? That he can't handle himself?

I stop in the middle of the hallway.

"This makes no sense," I say out loud. "He has to be lying. He bit his lip. Something is off."

A ginger freshman gives me a look of annoyance, or maybe it's bewilderment. I'm not sure. He says, "What?"

"Nothing." I wave him away. "Sorry. Thinking out loud."

Except for me bombing my world history test, none of this day makes any sense. So the big question here is, am I sane? And the obvious answer is that I am. I have evidence. There is a weird crystal in my pocket and there is a broken toilet seat in the bathroom. So, the second big question is, what happened to the bodies? How did someone know they were there? How did they get them out so quickly? And where did they put them? And what is this crystal about? Why is it important? And how did the alien girl know Pierce? Actually, that's way more than one second big question, but whatever. I have been through a traumatic experience and I'm allowed to have babble thoughts.

Actually, I have been through *three* traumatic experiences—bad world history test, alien attack and subsequent death, breaking up with Lyle in a friendship way and possibly a going-out way. Not to mention Seppie leaving town.

Yeah.

Today sucks.

Aliens. I don't even really understand anything about them other than they make my life much more complicated than it should be. Some are hot. Some appear human. Some don't. Some want humans to just be gone. Some don't really care. They aren't nice and neat and easily categorized. I guess nothing is. I mean, I thought Lyle was nice and neat and easily categorized. He went from best friend to kind of boyfriend to what? What is he now? Nothing?

My feet stop walking. I'm only by the front office. I haven't even made it outside yet, which is ridiculous. It shouldn't take me this long to just get out of the school.

And suddenly I want nothing more than to do exactly that, to just get out of the school. I want to get out of my life. I want to get out . . . get away . . . get anywhere . . . Anywhere other than here and this and now. Maybe this is how Lyle was feeling. Maybe this is how I made him feel.

So, I cover my mouth with my hand to give the impression that I really am about to puke. It helps hold the sob inside of me, anyway. I cover my mouth and start to run. Mrs. Sweet peeks out of the front office at me and says, sternly, "Go home, Mana. Go get some rest. Just go home."

But what is home?

A nothing place.

A house with nobody else.

I have no home.

CHAPTER 3

I have to double back because I realize I've forgotten half the stuff I need from my locker. I grab everything pretty quickly and then take a moment to breathe. Leaning against the row of lockers, I resist the urge to take out my phone and text China again. Instead, I pull the crystal out of my pocket. Despite the rumors, there are actually no surveillance cameras in our high school's hallways, and since everyone else is in class, this seems pretty safe. I don't think anyone will see me and if they do, I'm more likely to get in trouble for loitering in the halls without a hall pass than for having a medium-size, shiny rock in my hand.

The rock is warm, I guess from being next to my body. It's shaped like a prism with a broad base and a pointed end. The flat, dark surfaces don't really reflect light like a normal prism, but that's the best way my brain can describe it.

It vibrates in my hand.

"Cool," I say, because I am a master of words. "I wonder what you do exactly."

And then it levitates, just lifting a bit up and away. It hovers an inch above my hand and I grab for it. It bobs away.

"Seriously? You want to play tag?"

The prism lifts and spins, moving faster and faster in a circle as it hovers right by the sprinkler that's implanted in the ceiling in case of fire emergencies. I might let out a level-three curse word as I leap up to grab it. It darts away and as I land back on the floor, the prism makes a weird noise, sort of a buzzing. An image releases from it, or maybe projects is a better word? It's a guy, a big, golden guy, and he's talking to someone. The picture of him hovers about three feet off the floor. The image is pretty clear. I might let out another swear, level two this time.

"I think someone's watching me," he says. He has an accent that I can't quite place. His eyes are big and golden like his skin and his hair, but sad. He lifts up a box that has an address on it, tilting it toward me. I step closer, trying to make out the writing. He seems familiar somehow, but there's no reason why he should. His skin is clear and smooth, and he's got a pretty prominent brow ridge and a strong jaw. There is a lot of facial symmetry going on here. There's a beach behind him and some sort of . . . It's got to be an alien like Pierce, standing there next to this guy. It looks exactly like Pierce holding a surfboard that has a Nike swish and logo on it, all in black, and then beneath that this amazing psychedelic design. But as exciting as the surfboard is, I'm more intrigued by the golden guy and the sparkling alien next to him. Maybe this crystal thing is some sort of phone line? Or Skype? Or something?

I can't help stepping forward again, like getting closer is going to let me understand what I'm seeing a little bit better or something.

"Who are you?" I whisper. "Is that Pierce? *Pierce?*"

He jerks. "Did you hear that? Hey, Fey? Did you hear someone say something?"

Fey?

Is Pierce's name Fey? Or is this not Pierce at all? Isn't Fae her species? Someone makes a noise out of sight. And then there's another strange buzzing noise and the image disappears, replaced by the back of a head. It's another man. His hair is dark and short. He looks like he's in some sort of medical examining room. There is an empty hospital bed, but there are restraints at the sides and on the bottom of it, metal restraints that instantly scream out, *Sinister!* There's an IV and a medical monitor, but the walls look too barren to be even a hospital room. It's creepy.

"Hello?" I call out. Shudders move through my body and I instantly regret saying anything.

"You have it! Who are you?" He starts to turn, and just then the school bell rings. Doors slam open. This time I am 100 percent positive I level-four swear as I leap up and snatch the crystal out of the air. The image evaporates and I can't tell if the man ever turned to face me. I smash it back into my pocket and land right in front of a freshman. The image has vanished, but the freshman stares at me, open-mouthed.

"What the heck?" He manages to get this out but then his voice fails him. His lips move but no words come out.

"Were you on the ceiling?" the kid behind him asks.

"Seriously?" I say. "You guys are silly. I was just doing a front tuck. No cheer practice today. Have to keep up my mad skills."

Mad skills? I am such a mad dork, honestly. . . .

"Nice compliment, though. Much appreciated!" I fake punch the first kid in the arm. He sort of staggers backward because my punch turned out to pack way more power than either of us expected.

And then out of nowhere comes Principal Sweet's voice. "Ms. Trent! Did you just assault that boy?"

The freshman gives me horrified eyes. I give them right back to him. The guy behind him says, "No! She was stumbling for balance."

"She was trying to not fall over," first boy says, having found his voice just in time to lie to the principal.

I now love these random freshmen.

Principal Sweet clears her throat. "Ms. Trent. If you are so sick that you are losing your balance and vomiting in the restroom then I suggest you go home right this instant before you spread whatever contagion is inside of you to the rest of the student population. Do you understand me?"

"Of course," I say, suddenly even more cool with leaving. I want to tell Seppie about the crystal, about what just happened, even though I'm not supposed to tell anyone. I already told Lyle stuff. "Maybe September can drive me home? I'm not sure I'm well enough to drive myself."

Mrs. Sweet arches an eyebrow. She brushes some invisible lint off the lapel of her blazer.

"September has already left for her special camp." She clears her throat. "I'm surprised she didn't say goodbye."

My heart clenches.

"She did," I lie. "I just—I forgot. Sickness must have gone to my brain."

Mrs. Sweet pulls out her cell phone and starts texting, completely oblivious to my worries.

I was sure Seppie said she was leaving in a couple days or maybe tomorrow, but definitely not today, and I was sure she'd say a true goodbye, a goodbye that promised texting exchanges and Skype calls every other day and trading GIFs about cheering and . . . and . . . hugs. How could she just leave without doing any of that?

As I walk out of the school and down the hall, everything seems wrong and all my excitement over the crystal and possible Pierce sighting fades. Why would Seppie not tell me the whole truth about leaving? Why would Lyle suddenly be such a dork?

The thing is that you have best friends and you expect them to be there for you just like you want to be there for them. You don't expect them to be normal people and wig out on you when things get weird. You expect them to be honest. But expectations aren't reality, are they? I mean, that's why there are all those EXPECTATION VS. REALITY memes and a whole series about it on College Humor's website. Mom even quoted Shakespeare about expectations. I think it was from his play *All's Well That Ends Well*:

Oft expectation fails, and most oft there
Where most it promises; and oft it hits
Where hope is coldest, and despair most fits.

Which sort of means that expectations suck and when you expect a lot from people and they fail you, it hurts more than if you had no expectations at all.

I get that. I really do. And so I give up on expecting things from people or trusting them and head out the door of the school, crystal in pocket, ready to . . . ready to . . . I have no idea.

CHAPTER 4

nce I get out of the school and into the Subaru, I text Seppie. It is a long, pleading text that I type out in the front seat of the car and it ends with a question: SEPPIE, ARE YOU ALREADY GONE?

OF COURSE NOT, she types back. WHAT THE HELL?

What the hell is right. Mrs. Sweet wouldn't be wrong about that, would she?

MRS. SWEET SAID YOU WERE.

She writes, I AM SITTING RIGHT HERE IN LATIN CLASS. WHAT A WEIRDO.

ME?

YES. YOU. LOL. NO, I MEANT MRS. SWEET.

This is all so weird, but I have more important things to deal with.

I THINK LYLE HATES ME.

HE DOES NOT HATE YOU.

HE DOES. I text-explain everything that happened, leaving out the crystal. She just texts back that the alien thing is crazy and she's sorry she wasn't there to help and that boys are weird and there is probably another reason. If we had cheering today I would be able to talk to her in person about it and we could both sort of judge Lyle's interactions, but our coach said she has some sort of doctor's appointment about her quote-unquote lady parts, which was way TMI.

I am actually sort of stunned that Seppie is even texting during class. Something inside of me twists a little as I head down the access road away from the school. What if she isn't in class? What if Mrs. Sweet was right? What if Seppie is lying? I circle back to the school parking lot to see, feeling guilty even as I drive back into the lot. Friends aren't supposed to think their friends are lying. It goes against the friendship code.

The sky seems to heave above me, cloudy, watching. My head feels like it's stuck in a headlock, leaving my brain broken and helpless. This makes no sense. Nothing makes sense. The car's heater brings stale, warm air, but I don't want it. I want the reality of the heavy sky, the cold. I want to know what's real.

The school parking lot is mostly full, with only a few trucks and cars missing for those who have early dismissal. I was always jealous of the early dismissal kids, but Seppie and Lyle and I almost always carpooled anyway and they are way too college-tracked to ever get early dismissal status, which is basically for the kids who have to work part-time already to survive financially. They get out early so that they can start their shifts at McDonald's or Taco Bell. There is something inherently classist about all of this.

I cruise through the parking lot. I do not see Seppie's truck. I do spot Grayson Staggs, Lyle's best male friend. He's shortish and strongly made, wearing these beige Carhartt pants and hopping toward his diesel truck, which now runs on vegetable oil. He converted the engine himself and everything. I roll down my window even though it's cold out and yell his name. He trots right over. I love that about Grayson. He's smart but not judging. It's like he knows everything that is wrong with your insides and still loves you anyway.

"Hey, Grayson," I say.

"Hey, man."

Grayson calls people *man* no matter what gender they are. It's just stoner speak. He's not actually a stoner, though. He just talks that way. He watches stoner movies the way Lyle watches science fiction and it's just sort of seeped into his speech patterns, I guess.

"You see Seppie?" I ask.

"Naw, man. She took off before Latin. Said she had some special camp to go to or something."

My breath hitches in my chest. Again. I swear, my heart is not going to make it through this day. Seppie lied. Seppie blatantly lied to me. Did she honestly think I wouldn't know? Why would she do that?

I stare up at Grayson's earnest face, his wide-set eyes. He doesn't know anything about the alien stuff, doesn't know the real reason Lyle's parents are gone, or why Lyle and I are sleeping at Lyle's house half the time and mine the other. He doesn't know that the world is not as simple as we make it out to be. We've been lying to him, too.

Him and me. The clueless ones. And neither of us really knowing that we've been clueless.

"How about Lyle?" I ask. "He still here?"

"He bailed, too. You guys okay? You seem weird."

"Lyle is acting weird," I admit.

"It's a lot, you know, his mom getting arrested. His dad taking off. Your mom in the hospital. College next year. It's enough to screw up anyone's head, but you hold tight, man, wait it out. He's totally into you."

"You think so?" I stare up at his face like he's some Magic 8-Ball that's going to predict my future, give me all the right answers.

"I know so, man. I know so. Dude's just got a lot on his plate right now."

If Grayson only knew how much was on Lyle's plate, I think his head would explode.

"I keep trying to get him to take a gap year, hike the AT with me, you know? Boy is on the fast track to a life of white-collar boredom."

Grayson shudders just thinking about it. His eyes light up. "You should hike the AT with me, man. Graduate early and take off."

"It sounds tempting," I admit. "But I can't imagine graduating a year early."

Plus, my mom is in the hospital. I can't just abandon her.

"Drop out. Get your GED. I know you don't think you're super-stellar in the grades, but life's bigger than that, you know?"

He is so right. "I know."

"Think about it, man." He fist-bumps me. I fist-bump him back. He's got all sorts of little scars along the ridges of his thick knuckles. For a second, I wish he knew about everything—about the aliens, about me, about the threat—but I don't want to take away his happy innocence. "And don't worry about Lyle. He's still into you. Guys *are* weird. Take it from me, man. I'm a guy. I should know. Totally weird." He smiles all hearty and ho-ho and I can imagine him seventy years old and dressed up as Santa, having the best time with it. He leans in my window. "It'll be cool when he gets back."

I put my foot on the brake.

"Gets back?"

"Yeah, man. From running camp."

"Lyle's going to running camp?" I ask. I narrow my eyes. This does not make sense. "There are no running camps in December."

"Yeah. Like two weeks or something. Shit. Did he not tell you? No wonder he's acting so flake. Sorry, man. He probably . . . Yeah . . . wow . . ."

We say goodbye and I'm not sure what to think. Both Lyle and Seppie left early. Seppie lied in her text exchange to me, which is not something she would normally do.

Rolling up my window, I drive out of the parking lot and try not to freak out, but the truth is this has not been the greatest of days.

"What do I do now?" I ask the car.

The car does not answer, which is one normal thing, I guess. I keep moving forward. It's the only thing I can think to do even if I don't know where exactly moving forward is bringing me. It's something.

I decide that I deserve some quiet, alone time even though I'm an extrovert. I just want a tiny bit of peace, so I head to a place I loved when I was little.

I don't go to the forest much anymore, only about once every other week. It isn't just that it's so cold out now. It's more that I don't feel 100 percent safe anywhere and the little piece of forest at the edge of our subdivision has memories, dark memories, of when the Wendigo tried to kill Lyle and me in my house, that night when it all started. It makes me remember darkness and fear.

But since it is still daylight, thanks to my early school release, I drive there before I head to the hospital. After I park and lock the car, I step into the trees. The sky is not the tornado darkness of my dreams, but the overcast gray of an oncoming snowstorm. The leaves will be covered soon. The snow will cover them, hide them beneath its whiteness. The world is full of secrets. Only the sky lets you know what's about to happen, warns you that it's about to storm.

The trees stand like tall stakes for giant vampires. My feet crunch on the half-covered leaves and pine needles. Snow flurries have skimmed their surface and the cold has hardened them. In the distance, I think I spot a shadow of a dog, or a raccoon. I wave *hi*. It feels good here, normal. My breath comes out in little puffs, the heat of it turning to vapor in the cold air. I am not a big fan of the cold, but right now it feels so real, so bitter that I kind of welcome it. It's like it's reminding me that I'm alive.

Once I'm a decent distance from the car, without even really planning to, I lift the crystal out of my pocket and let it go. The crystal spins and an image appears. It's that guy again—running.

"Hello?" I squeak into the air.

"Mana! Are you out there? Your name's Mana, right? I'm James Henry Smith. Fey told me your name. Look. I can't talk." His breath is coming in rapid bursts. His eyes are dilated. "Something's chasing me. Fey said to tell you that . . . they want to find you . . . Be—"

He screams.

A bright blue figure appears, obstructing my view. Claws fill the vision.

The scene switches but I'm still yelling for this guy I don't know. He knew my name. Fey *must* be Pierce. And this guy? James Henry Smith. He might be dead.

Because of me, says the voice in my head.

And my stomach spirals into despair even as the crystal scene changes again to that medical room. I snatch it out of the air. I don't want to see that. Instead, I lean against a tree and try to slow down my breath, but worry for James Henry Smith pushes my panic to right about the edge of unsafe. *James Henry?*

My brain just keeps repeating his name.

Please be okay.

Mana . . .

It's a voice. His voice. In my thoughts.

Be careful.

And then it fades away just as my phone rings. The sound makes me jump about seven feet in the air. The screen reads *Seppie.* I answer.

"Seppie! Where are you? Why are you lying to me? What the heck is going on?" My questions come out in a colossal blur, but she talks right over me.

"Mana. Please be careful. A man is searching for you. Whatever you have, you need to hide it. Hide yourself, too, maybe."

"Seppie! Where are you? Are you okay? What are you even talking about?" I didn't tell her about the crystal, but she knows I have something.

"Yes. Just be careful."

"Tell me what's going on."

"I will. Not now."

She hangs up. I call her right back. She does not answer. I text her. She does not answer. I angry-text her. She does not answer. I pleading-text her. She does not answer. I swear, she's being as bad as China. But what if it's not on purpose? She could be in danger and I have no idea where she is or anything.

The woods feel horrible again, dark and foreboding. No squirrels bounce around on tree branches. No birds flit and chirp. Nothing. It's almost as bad as my apocalypse dream. I stash the crystal back in my coat pocket despite the temptation to try to connect with James Henry Smith again. But what if he's dead? I am not sure I can deal with that at the moment.

Something moves.

I freeze.

In the distance, maybe half a mile away, something thunders through the trees. It's big and immense and obviously alien. My heart accelerates. It's not heading my way; I don't think it sees me, but I bet it's looking for me. A dog barks in the expanse.

The world suddenly feels even smaller, even less safe, and I walk fast to my car, suddenly desperate to get to the hospital and check on my mom and get away from the alien stomping through the woods. The entire ride I worry about James Henry Smith and if my using that crystal put him in danger somehow. I worry about it more than Seppie saying that someone is looking for me. I'd rather face danger and get it over with than have it keep lurking in bathrooms and dreams, making me tense and anxious from what seems like a perpetual wait.

I pull over and text Seppie again.

Nothing.

Again.

I roll down the windows, scan the woods for that large alien thing, which I'm trying not to get all scared about, and I'm truly pushing my fear down, into the pits of me, so that it doesn't take over. When

I let my fear take over, I make bad decisions. That's what Mom always says. I text China even though I doubt it's any use.

AN ALIEN IS LOOKING FOR ME. JUST SO YOU KNOW.

Despite all my worries, I try to refocus my thoughts while I drive the cold, snow-dusted streets to the hospital and think about how this makes no sense for Seppie and Lyle to be abandoning me now, or ever. That's not who we are.

About three weeks ago, Seppie and Lyle and I went out one night, late, and it was dark. I'd come back from visiting my mom at the hospital and was pretty stressed out because I wasn't hearing back from China. We hiked up Uncanoonuc Mountain's north peak, following the ski trails that were abandoned before the area was ever opened to the public. Environmentalists were worried about the impact on the ecosystem. Unfortunately they worried about that after the people making the ski area already knocked over a lot of the trees. It's ironic because the south peak is now covered in transmitting facilities for a whole bunch of the local broadcasters, which seems worse than ski slopes. The highest peak is only about 1,300 feet, but it's enough sometimes to feel like you could reach the sky.

There is a panoramic view from that mountain, mostly because the area around it lacks any elevation. Above us, the sky went on forever and we could find constellations and satellites, glistening, blinking out ancient signals. What stars hosted the planets our scientists so desperately sought? Where are the aliens from? Can we even see them? All these questions danced above us, but it wasn't a horrible feeling. It was more peaceful, knowing how tiny we were, knowing that we were together in the mystery. Just the day before, I had read that there was still no trace of life on other planets, no sustainable environments. Maybe that was why we were so important, such a highlight on the alien highway. Maybe it was because our planet is so cool, so full of water and oxygen and minerals, teeming with life and bacteria and growth.

Seppie brought sleeping bags because she likes to be prepared. She even spread them out at perfect angles, all positioned exactly next to each other. I had the middle sleeping bag and I flattened out on it. It wasn't much of a barrier between me and the cold, bumpy ground, but it was enough.

"The sky is so big," Lyle whispered. I held his hand and I grabbed Seppie's, too. Hers was warm. His? Not so much. Lyle always has cold hands. It's part of his weirdness, we always thought, but then we learned it's actually part of his species. His earlobes are the same way.

"This place feels haunted," I said. "Not in a bad way. I love you guys."

"Are we supposed to be looking for UFOs or are we having one of those group therapy sessions that always happen once you say that you love us?" Seppie asked. She was serious. "I'm not super into those. I hate all the feeling, 'let's grow together' talks."

I ignore her, because I know that she doesn't really mean it in a jerk-way, and ask, "What do you think it means, that the aliens made me as a weapon?"

"It means that you're badass." Seppie squeezed my hand.

"Seriously, though."

"I am serious." She sighed and paused. Lyle didn't even interrupt, which was sort of earth-shatteringly abnormal. "You are badass. You have skills. We don't know them all, but you bound around like a kangaroo on steroids. You have sweet, sweet, tumbling abilities. You are stronger than you should be, obviously, and you can kind of hear the thoughts of some aliens."

"But not all," Lyle interjected. "Thank God."

Seppie laughed. "Imagine if you heard Lyle the Crocodile's thoughts all the time. It'd be *Doctor Who* this. *You're so hot* that. Blah, blah, blah."

"Not nice," I scolded.

"Super not nice," Lyle added. "But true."

Seppie laughed again and for a second, I worried that she and Lyle weren't going to put real thought into this and just sort of kid it away, but then she went, "It means that you're special but that you don't quite understand how."

"Which is sort of a theme for all of humanity. Myself included, despite my alien DNA, thank you very much." Lyle sighed. "I mean, all your questions can apply to me, too. Why am I an alien? What does that mean?"

"You're an alien because your parents are aliens," Seppie countered. "It's biological and understandable in the little-picture way, whereas Mana is engineered for a purpose, a big-picture purpose."

"True." Lyle let go of my hand. He moved hair out of his eyes. "But it still is weird and hard and frustrating."

"Try being the boring, black, human sidekick with no special powers," Seppie said.

"You are super-special and not boring at all." I rolled on my side to face her. "That is the stupidest thing you've ever said in your whole life."

"I just feel sort of regular," she admitted.

A tiny tear scrolled down her cheek. I wiped it away. Seppie never tears up. She made an excuse about the cold impacting her eyes. We scoffed.

"She's just used to catching us and saving our asses and you just saved hers. Role reversal is hard to get used to." Lyle spewed this off like there was no emotion behind it.

I studied Seppie. "Is that true?"

"Possibly. But that's not the point right now. The point right now is, what does it mean that you are this weapon that was subverted and taken back to humanity? What can you do? What will you do?"

Lyle said, "It's fascinating, really."

"It's me. It's not fascinating. It's terrifying," I whispered.

"Most fascinating things are."

We'd spent the rest of the night there, staring up at the stars. Seppie and Lyle pretended to be sleeping over at other people's houses (mine and Grayson's, respectively). I didn't have to pretend anything. We danced. We raged. We drank things that we probably shouldn't have drank. We went feral in the coldness of the night. We sang. We pondered. We shook our fists at the sky. We were tired and angry and sad and exuberant all at once because the world, our world, had a million adventures in store for us and we would conquer them together, best friends, forever friends; we made the promises of innocent devils and we didn't think for a second that those promises would not be true.

No. I will make sure that they are true. Anger fills me. Whatever Lyle and Seppie are up to, it has got to be for a reason. I'm going to find out that reason as soon as I visit my mom and somehow make sure that the Australian guy is okay, and maybe after a snack. But it will happen. Friends don't let friends blow them off and keep secrets. It's just not in the code.

CHAPTER 5

Since the events first began, I've been reading as much as I can about aliens. I have no idea if the nonfiction books are actually fiction or if the fiction books are actually nonfiction. But there are themes that run through all of them. And one of those themes is that not all aliens are alike.

In *Encounters with Star People*, a researcher named Dr. Ardy Sixkiller Clarke interviews indigenous people of North America about their encounters with aliens. In one interview she talks to a one-hundred-year-old woman who had been visited by "star people" all her life. A week before she died, the woman was visited by other star people who looked and acted differently than the others from before. They had long fingers and big shoulders and glittery black pants. One of the star people cut a piece of her hair and asked her why she lived so long. Inexplicably, she was suddenly afraid of them, these random hair-cutting aliens who were so cranky and free with their scissors. She had spent one hundred years looking forward to the star people's visits and a week before she died, that all changed.

And that's the thing. There are so many aliens. I have lived all these years—okay, not close to one hundred—and not known they existed. My mother actually hunted them down and I still had no clue. My best friend turned out to be one of them, which explains his freaky, effortless running skills.

Refusing to feel dull and broken about Seppie and Lyle, or China never texting me back, I drive my mom's car to the hospital and park outside because I visit Mom every day, no matter what. The afternoon is white and cold. Clouds cover the sky, cloaking it at great heights. The parking lot smells of exhaust and cold air as I stride across it. The air bites my ankles, nips at my cheeks. A dog barks in the distance. The crystal feels large and obvious in my coat pocket. I don't want to wrap my hand around it in case it starts projecting images again. It's warm. Should a rock be warm? Is it even a rock? What if it's some weird alien life form that will transform into a talking yeti that spews out toxic poop, killing all of New Hampshire?

My brain is weird.

But everything feels dangerous. I almost hear something at the edge of my brain whisper, *Come here.*

What?

There is no answer, just a tugging from that far corner of my brain. As I stride across the parking lot, I search for threats— anything and everything could be one. A telephone pole could topple down. A car could gun it and rev forward. A man could aim a rifle. A woman could flash a knife. An orc alien thing could thump out from behind a Dumpster. Nothing happens.

I've gotten paranoid.

China always says paranoia keeps you alive. But Seppie always says that paranoia keeps you paranoid.

They are both probably right.

I might be paranoid, but I have to protect this crystal thing. It's important somehow. And the last time I had to protect something, look how that turned out: my mom is in a hospital, perpetually unconscious.

Inside the hospital, the light is fluorescent and fake. Salmon-painted walls line long, shiny hallways. The nurses at the stations greet me by name and one even says, "School out early today?"

"Sort of." I shrug in response. She is kind enough not to ask a follow-up question.

My mother's small body barely registers in the hospital bed. Her hair has been recently washed. Her monitors beep and hum, which is supposedly reassuring, but to me the noise is a reminder of her condition—not dead, barely alive . . . waiting. What if the waiting never ends? That's the question, really.

I perch on a chair and shimmy it closer to her. "Hey."

She doesn't respond. She hasn't responded for weeks. She is almost in a coma, but not quite. She is officially unconscious and non-responsive. It's easier to just say *coma*.

"School was bad today," I whisper, reaching out a finger to touch the skin of her hand. It's so dry. It's almost flaking. I grab some of the hospital moisturizer off the side bureau and start slathering it on, but it won't do much. The dryness is coming from the inside. She's dehydrated despite the fluids pumping into her. "How is the hospital doing? Any exciting nurse gossip? Cool visitors? Epiphanies about the state of mankind?"

I babble to her, tell her the events of my day, especially about the crystal, glossing over the Lyle incident, but then giving up and explaining it all. I tell her about the aliens, about Lyle and Seppie, how I appreciate her having the bills on automatic payment, but I don't know how much money is in her checking account, and then I tell her about Lyle and Seppie again, focusing on Lyle because at least Seppie said she was going away while Lyle just shoved me away. And I'm not sure how to process that. Or the obvious lie that has to be behind them both going away to camps on the same day, suddenly . . . or at least suddenly to me.

"I told you that boy wasn't good enough for you." The voice comes from behind me, startling me so much that I drop the moisturizer bottle. Liquid globs out all over the floor.

Patrick Kinsella, also known as China, also known as text ignorer, moves forward, grimacing. "Sorry."

He yanks some paper towels out of a metal wall dispenser and then squats next to me, helping me to clean up the mess. His sunglasses shroud his eyes.

"It'll be a well-moisturized floor," he says as if nothing has happened, like he hasn't ghosted me for weeks. He just says it like the confident bastard that he is.

Wonderful, I think. *Now he shows up.*

I am so angry and shocked and, despite everything, sort of relieved somehow to see him that I don't know what to say. I haven't said anything. Not even hi.

China is a muscular guy with dark skin and dark eyes and black hair. He stands way taller than my five feet nothing, and has the well-built body of a professional soldier, like a Greek statue that hasn't been broken in between trips to European museums. He carries with him the smell of leather and man. He crumples all the paper towels into a ball and tosses it into the wastebasket without even looking over his shoulder at where it lands behind him. It swooshes in perfectly.

"Two points?" he asks in his deep voice that makes questions into statements.

"Three." It was a good shot. I'll give him that.

"So, heard you talking to your mom. What's with the boyfriend?" He stands up to his full height and the smell of leather jacket recedes a little bit. He walks to the end of the room, shuts the door to the hallway, and comes back to stand next to me. "He's always here with you."

"You know this how?"

He doesn't answer.

"You've been watching me?" I move to put the moisturizer back and check on my mom. He doesn't have to answer. The answer is obvious. After a minute of silence, I say, "Are you here now because Lyle isn't here and you don't want to involve him even though you promised me you would, or are you here now because of what happened this afternoon?"

"What happened this afternoon? You and Lyle having your tiff?" He takes the moisturizer and squirts some out into his hand. Gently, he picks up my mother's hand in his and starts to spread the moisture in circles. It's tender. It's surprising.

"You don't know?" I scrutinize his face, but it's hard to read his expression because of the sunglasses. "You *really* don't know?"

"Nope." His voice sounds amused. "I really don't know."

"An alien tried to kill me. Another tried to save me. Both died." I don't mention the crystal. I am going to keep it simple for now. That way I can figure out what information to share. "And I saw another in the woods."

His posture shifts into a more erect stance. "What? Where?"

"The deaths? School bathroom."

"And the type of aliens?"

I give him the rundown on what actually happened. I don't know the kinds and names of all the aliens, but like I said before, I've been reading up on all things alien. Describing them is easy. Explaining about the toilet seat maneuver is embarrassing.

"That was fast thinking," he says, surprising me.

"Wait. Did you just praise me?"

His lips twitch at the right corner. He doesn't stop me until I get to the part about Lyle and me returning and the bodies being gone.

"Gone?"

"Yep. Just gone. They put the toilet seat back, too, but forgot to actually bolt it back down."

"So, it was a rush job."

"I had barely left. It was a super-rush job. Who would do that?" I ask.

He wipes his hands together, removing the extra moisturizer, I guess. "So many. None. Everyone. There are a million answers to that question, Mana."

"So, what is the most likely answer?"

"Are you hungry?" He reaches out a hand to me. To do this he has to reach across my mother's body, which seems awkward and wrong, so I don't take it.

I admit, "Yeah."

I can't remember when I last ate. Lyle can always remember when he's last eaten. Lyle is food focused.

"Late lunch is the first step to our answer, then." He wiggles his fingers.

"I'll agree if you take off your sunglasses inside."

He laughs. "I'm about to go outside. I'll just put them on again."

He wiggles his fingers one more time. Giving up, I take them. I have never voluntarily touched him before. I don't explode or catch fire all over my mother, so that's nice, but then I let go, bending over my mom, kissing the dry flaky skin of her forehead.

"I love you," I whisper. "I'll be right back."

When I stand up straight again, China is staring at me with a strange expression on his face. His brow furrows, but his eyes remain wide.

"Do you say that every time?" he asks. "Say 'I'll be right back'?"

"Yep."

"So do I."

"That doesn't make me forgive you for not answering my texts."

"You sent three a day." He self-corrects, "A minimum of three a day."

"Whatever."

"It wasn't time yet."

"And now it is?"

He sighs and averts his gaze. "Possibly."

A long time ago, Lyle, Seppie, and I had a huge argument over why Goofy the dog could talk in the Disney universe, but Pluto the dog couldn't. Lyle said it was because one was a pet and one was an equal. Seppie said that none of it made sense. Half the animals in Disney could talk and half couldn't, even if they were pets. She used Pascal in *Tangled* and the mice in *Cinderella* and Percy in *Pocahontas* as examples. I just thought it was irrelevant. "You either believe or you don't," I said.

They didn't get it.

We were at cheer practice, running laps inside the school hallways because it was winter and snowing outside. Lyle was being kind and staying with us instead of sprinting ahead effortlessly. We were pounding up the stairs, our normal, happy trio.

"You can't just believe that one dog can talk and another can't," Seppie insisted. "Any more than you can believe that the dragon in *Mulan* or the fish in *The Little Mermaid* can talk."

"So you're saying you can't believe any animated creatures can talk?" Lyle asked.

"Exactly."

We got to the hall straightaway past the foreign language rooms. It stank up there.

"Then you can't enjoy the movies or the cartoons." He was flabbergasted.

Seppie threw her hands up in the air. "How can you possibly enjoy something that you know is impossible? That makes no logical sense?"

"It's not impossible. Nothing is impossible," he countered.

I had tuned them out. I don't even remember who—if anyone— won the argument. What had changed since then? We never kept secrets. We told one another everything.

Not everything, I reminded myself.

Lyle and I didn't tell Seppie about when the Wendigo appeared at my house and tried to eat us. We wanted her to have fun and go to a party and then when everything went to hell, when we realized about the chip and the aliens, we still didn't tell her because we wanted to protect her, to keep her safe. We did tell her eventually, when it was impossible not to tell her, but we kept it secret as long as we could.

But that couldn't be what was happening now. We all know about the aliens. Lyle is one. I'm just making excuses for them because I still love them both, no matter what.

China and I make it all the way outside the hospital before he says, "Are you still in?"

"In?" I stop beneath the awning, standing on the bland concrete that has salt thrown down on the icy patches. The salt has melted the ice away, and even though its work is done, it remains there.

China sighs as if my question is a real question and not just me buying time. "Do you want to still help me if it's okay with the higher-ups?"

"Three texts a day during which I beg doesn't make you think I'm in?"

"You could have changed your mind."

"Because why?"

"Because I took forever to respond. Because Lyle is being weird. Because of the bathroom incident. People change their minds all the time."

I creep over to the salty mixture, touch it with my toe. That salt had a reason and then it didn't. I have a reason, too. My mom had a reason. That girl who died in the bathroom had a reason. Even that orc-Shrek-alien-of-evil had a reason. Once you know your reason, is there really a point in fighting it? Before the salt dissolves the ice so that people don't slip, what does the salt do? It just stays in the bucket, waiting. I am not into waiting.

"Yeah," I tell him. "Yeah. I'm still in."

He claps his hands together and rubs them. "Okay, first stop is food. Come on."

"Are you paying?" I ask.

"Of course."

Even if I did have a good handle on how much money is in Mom's bank account and how much on her credit card line, free food is not something I would ever argue with. I stand staring out at the hospital parking lot. An ambulance pulls in to the emergency room driveway. A nurse and a doctor rush out of the hospital doors. Paramedics jump out of the ambulance, open the back, pull out a wheeled stretcher with a person on it. So many people hurt all the time. So much violence. So much pain. I am tired of doing nothing, of being helpless, of just barely hanging on, of not knowing exactly what is going on, ever, of never being in control.

"Let's take my car," I tell China.

His lips twitch. "If that's what you'd prefer."

"Definitely."

Something grumbles from behind the ambulance. I freeze because the grumble sounds exactly like the creature in the woods. The EMTs have already shut the door and headed inside, but the ambulance shakes and then topples over onto its side. I scream. China jumps in front of me. I move him out of the way. One second later, an alien just like the one in the bathroom is standing on top of the ambulance. It has pieces of tree branches sticking out of its toes.

"That's what it looked like!" I yell.

"Stand back. I've got this." China pulls a spray bottle out of his pocket. It looks like a cleaner bottle with red liquid inside it, but he yanks the spray nozzle and pulls at it until it's about three feet long. "Watch out for the tongue!"

The tongue lashes at us. I tuck up and to the left. China dives right, rolling on the asphalt, right over the NO PARKING line, and shoots. The nasty-smelling red liquid sprays out and hits the orc's tongue. It recoils. He shoots again and it hits the monster directly on one of its four eyes. It rumbles and bounces and screams.

"Duck!" he yells. I've dived behind one of the hospital's support posts and manage to miss the spray as the alien explodes.

China has taken shelter behind a trash receptacle. Only a bit of alien flesh lands in his hair. He wipes it off and tucks the spray nozzle back into place and then pushes the bottle into his pocket. He is still wearing his sunglasses.

"You had that with you because?" I blurt, hands on my hips.

"I heard there was an orc around here." He is nonchalantly using his cell phone to search for alien pieces. He finds an eyeball on his shoulder and flicks it off.

I stand there with him and demand, "Before I told you? You knew this? Is that why you're here?"

He shrugs. "Pretty much. Still want to take your car?"

I stare at the exploded alien all over the ground for one more second. "Absolutely."

CHAPTER 6

We head to a place called the Side Street Café, and I order a hummus and olive tapenade plate with home-made pita chips and a salad and a side order of sweet potato fries. China, to his credit, does not make any snarky "hungry" comments, which I appreciate, but the waitress's eyes widen as my order expands and expands.

"And a soy shake," I finish, closing the menu shut finally. "Please. Thanks!"

I beam at her and sit back in the chair, my spirits buoyed by the thought of food, a lot of food, a lot of good food.

China orders a fish burger, which is totally not what I would have expected. When the waitress leaves, he says, "Tell me what happened with Lyle."

"Are you being my dad?" I squint at him like that will somehow allow me to read his intentions. It seems weird that he cares about what's going on with me and Lyle. He's not exactly Mr. Empathy.

He takes the knife and taps the handle on the table. Then he reaches up, taking off his sunglasses, revealing his dark eyes, which are warm and a little sad. "No, I'm being me."

So, I tell him the Lyle parts that I left out of the story, only pausing when the waitress brings water and my soy shake. She tries to flirt with China. China is oblivious, which makes me feel bad for the waitress. Flirting with obliviousness is never fun. Believe me, I know.

He clears his throat and leans forward after I've explained it all. "I hate to suggest this, but maybe it wasn't Lyle. Maybe it was a shapeshifter, like the ones we've met before."

A tiny muscle at the edge of his eye twitches. He rubs at it with his napkin as my heart sort of stops. The door to the café opens with a creak. Cold air bursts inside. The door shuts. "I never even thought about that."

"It's possible, or he may just be being a douche nozzle." China accepts the plate of food from the waitress, making eye contact. She giggles. Giggles! I am so worried about my gender. I want to tell her that it isn't worth it. Guys will kiss you and then say they can't handle it. They will be your best friend and then they'll get yelled at by the principal and it will be all over. Guys are not worth giggling over, especially if you've only just met them. But I do not preach as she sets my shake and food plate down, I just wait.

Once she's gone again, I say, standing up, "We should go find him. If that isn't Lyle, then we have to make sure the real Lyle is okay."

He doesn't move. "Mana. When was the last time you ate?"

I don't answer because two days ago isn't the sort of answer he'd want to hear.

He points his fork at me and then my plate and then back at me again. "We need to eat first . . . I have suggested it because it's good to look at all possibilities, but it's highly doubtful Lyle was Not Lyle. He wouldn't have pushed you away if he was. So, let's not worry about him as a number one priority until we've dealt with other things. Seppie? Same deal. Plus, someone is meeting us here. Orders from the top brass. They think he might have some important intel."

"Who?" I ask, torn between leaving and eating.

"Me. Sorry, I'm early."

I turn around. The man is around Six foot five and built like a pro wrestler, all muscle and bulk, buzz-cut hair. "Tim Wharff."

He reaches out his hand. I shake it. He doesn't crush my fingers, so that gives him a lot of bonus points. His last name is Wharff. That sounds just like a Klingon name of a major character in the *Star Trek* universe. I didn't realize people even had that for a last name. Lyle would be very into this in an excited way.

Lyle.

My food doesn't come across as appetizing, all of a sudden.

"Don't mind her. She just lost her boyfriend," China explains, motioning for Wharff to sit down and then making a motion for the server to come back to the table.

"Did they take him?" Wharff asks, swallowing the chair with his bulk.

"Take him?" I ask.

"Abduct him," Wharff explains, grabbing a napkin and daintily spreading it across his lap.

I almost choke on my shake. "No."

"Dead?" His eyes meet mine. The pupils are a bit wobbly. They jump around.

"No! He just—He just—ah . . ."

"He dumped her," China explains for me in his lovely tactful way. "Or maybe not. I'm not a hundred percent convinced it was actually him. Or that it was an actual breakup. Or that they were technically dating."

I stare at my food, somehow losing my appetite even more. "It was him."

Wharff sips his water. All his actions seem slow and deliberate. "He is a fool then."

"I've always said that," China agrees.

"I'm not cool with talking about him when he's not here," I say. "It's mean."

"He dumps her and she's worried about being mean? When he can't even hear it?" Wharff places the glass on the table again, delicately. "That's a whole lot of kindness in one person."

"Too much, if you ask me," China grumps.

Luckily, the server comes back. Wharff orders two cheeseburgers, a salad with blue cheese dressing, a milk shake, orders me another shake, adds a piece of apple pie, and asks for both regular fries and sweet potato fries. The waitress gives him this face like she's totally appreciative of his appetite and makes one of those flirty comments about big men and big whatever, which is *so* inappropriate. China rolls his eyes. Wharff, however, doesn't even really notice. It's like he's used to it or doesn't care or both. When their little interchange is done, he settles in and tells us to eat our food before it gets cold, but I can't do that because it's too impolite and my mother would kill me. China dives right in.

The men make small talk about the New England Patriots and football teams for a while and I zone out, remembering the time Lyle and I went to a diner and it turned out to not be Lyle, but a shape-shifting alien. I had escaped in the nick of time through the ceiling of the restroom. I fell through the kitchen and fled to the street, where I eventually found the real Lyle and China. Good times. Not really, but I'm trying to hold on to the remnants of a positive mental attitude. I used to be positive all the time before I knew about the aliens.

The waitress serves Wharff. He is enthusiastic about his food and she trots off happy. We all dig in and even though my own meal isn't chicken or anything, it tastes brilliant, as does the smooth, cold vanilla soy shake. I guess my appetite has returned.

Wharff eyes me eating. "Are you not feeding her?"

"I haven't seen her in a while," China replies.

Wharff harrumphs like that is not a good enough answer. Once he's ravished one burger and half the salad, he tells us that he's been abducted before.

"I know that you believe. I wouldn't be here if you didn't, so I'm going to skip with the precursors and I'm only going to tell you this story one time. If you mock me, I leave." He smiles. "With my burger, of course."

His grin seems forced, a bit of bravado, and I suddenly feel for this big man who was obviously once helpless and probably afraid. It's hard to feel helpless and afraid. I totally get this feeling.

"We won't mock you," I say. I reach across the table and touch his hand, trying to give him some comfort even as the crystal vibrating slightly in my pocket distracts me. "I promise."

He seems reassured and begins to tell us a story, pausing only when the server comes too near. He tells us that he drives a truck in between stints in his MMA career, and explains to me that MMA stands for mixed martial arts. Men and women fight each other for money, kind of like professional wrestling with more realism or boxing with legal kicking. Anyway, he had a bit of MMA-enforced bad luck to make the season more dramatic and he was driving a Walmart truck for a couple months to help make his story more sympathetic.

"They want me to come back as the underdog, the everyman's hero. Walmart trucker fits into that persona," he says between bites of lettuce.

One night he's driving the eighteen-wheeler down the long, deserted stretch of highway in north-central Maine between Augusta, the state capital, and Bangor, which has an airport and a mall or something. There are no lights on the interstate up there, and barely a car. He noticed an orange glow ahead, a reddish-orange glow, and he started to slow the truck down, figuring there had been an accident and some cars were on fire. He got on the radio and asked if anyone knew anything.

"All I got was static," he says. "And then I'm over the hill and I see it. It's hovering right over the highway, maybe two or three feet above the ground."

"It?" I ask.

"The craft. It's circular and huge, covers more than both lanes of the highway, and there are a lot of lights on it, little lights, mostly white, some red. Looking at it is like looking at a little city, you know?

When you look at a city from on top of a mountain. That's what it's like."

He pauses and takes a drink of his water. Then changes his mind and goes for the milk shake. I sip mine, too, slurping it through the straw and then apologizing for the noise. I don't think either of the guys actually notices the noise or the apology, honestly. China is super-focused on this Wharff guy's story and I can't blame him because the guy is a compelling, charismatic storyteller.

Wharff's eyes close for a second as if he's cut up remembering. The chatter of the restaurant seems to ease its way back into my ears. Other people at other tables chew and talk and clank their silverware and slurp their shakes just like I did. The world continues. People continue.

He starts talking again. "I brake the truck. Because? Well, what else am I going to do. I can't turn around. I wasn't about to try to run through it. There were three or four figures outside the craft. They were moving around it. It reminded me of how you spot check the outside of an airplane, but I don't know if that's what they were really doing or if that's just me trying to put human reason onto what I saw, you know?"

"We all want things to make sense. It's normal to do that," China says.

"Yeah . . . yeah . . ." Wharff picks up a french fry, dabs it in ketchup. "I was pretty much freaked at this point. I couldn't make out any features on the figures, but they were human-shaped, just not quite right. Their heads were wrong. They were elongated and their shoulders were tiny, more like Mana here than a normal person."

I am not sure whether or not to be offended but I decide it doesn't matter that I don't have normal-person shoulders. There are worse things. Believe me, I know.

He keeps talking. He didn't know what to do, but he was scared. Really scared. He fully stopped the truck, reached into his glove compartment and pulled out the gun he kept there, a .357—whatever that is. He flashed his lights at the craft.

"I don't know what I thought I was doing. Maybe that I'd scare them off, the way you scare a deer. Yeah." He laughs. "I'm an idiot."

"It was a good idea," I say, because I feel bad for him, not because it was actually a good idea.

"You're a nice kid, Mana. A real good kid." He sighs. "They took me."

I stop chewing my own french fry. They took me, too, once, but I don't remember it. Maybe that's why China is letting me hear this story. Maybe it's so I can understand my own. Maybe it's so I don't feel so alone, because you feel so alone when something like this happens to you.

"They took me," he repeats. "One of the figures started walking toward the truck. I tried to shoot it. Nothing happened. I tried to run, to scramble out of the truck, but I was frozen. Next thing I know there's this thing in front of me, wearing a glittery, skintight unitard-type thing. Not glittery in a princess toddler girl way, but just sort of sparkling."

"What color?" China asks.

"Black."

"A unitard like dancers wear?" I stutter out and feel instantly bad because the expression on Wharff's face is guarded and embarrassed. "I'm just trying to imagine it," I babble in my attempt to make it less awkward. "Sorry. I don't meant to sound offensive or anything. I totally believe you."

And I do. I do believe this stranger. I don't trust anyone, but I believe him, and for a second I have to wonder if belief is the first step in trust or vice versa.

He sucks his lips in toward his mouth before he talks again. His face twists into something stern and resolved and full of anguish all at once. "I know. I know it sounds . . . It sounds ridiculous."

We both start trying to make him feel better and assure him that we have seen things much more ridiculous than an alien in a glittery unitard-type thing (alien acid tongues, alien Shrek monsters killed by toilet seats), but it isn't until I say that wrestlers wear skin-tight stuff like that, too, that he finally calms down enough to finish his story.

"So, he walks toward me and I can't move. I just literally can't move. A second before, I had grabbed my gun, got ready to open the door and run, since the truck wasn't working . . . and then . . . nothing. I focused everything I had on pulling the trigger to that gun and my freaking finger did not move one inch. Not one freaking millimeter, honestly. Excuse my French." He laughs, shaking his head, but it isn't a happy laugh. "The only good thing I can say about the whole thing is at least I didn't piss myself. Excuse my French again."

I make a face so he knows that he doesn't have to "excuse his French" around me, whatever the heck that expression is even supposed to mean. He gobbles down some pie and then tells us, the next thing he knows, he's walking out of the truck, the alien right next to him guiding him along toward the spaceship. He didn't feel like he was moving himself. It was more like sleepwalking or dream walking.

"But I wasn't dreaming," he insists.

He continues into the spacecraft, a V-shaped door opens up, and then next thing he knows he is in a pale metal room and the alien is telling him not to panic, that everything is fine.

He laughs at himself. "I said that everything was not fine because I was being abducted on an alien spaceship. That got the alien's attention and he said that they weren't taking me anywhere and so they weren't technically abducting me. I said that any sort of entrapment for any period of time against a person's will is technically abducting. The alien said I was smarter than the average human." He lifts his shoulders. "I guess he meant that as a compliment, but I was sort of pissed off on behalf of the entire species, you know?"

I know.

"This whole time, are you guys talking English?" I ask.

"No. It's more like he's in my head with me. That's how I even knew he was sort of male. I didn't see his di—his genitalia or anything. It was more like the sense of him." He examines his fork. "So, I ask him what he is doing this for, why he has me. And he says that they thought they had a tiny glitch with the ship and had to make sure that it was okay. They took me because I was in the wrong place at the wrong time and saw them. He said that they were scientists and that they don't interfere with life on other planets, but . . ."

China finally perks up. "But?"

"But that they were worried about ours because of other aliens interfering. I was like, 'What other aliens?' And he said, 'There are only five violent federations in this galaxy. Yours is one of them, but yours is by far the most primitive. Others are interested in seeing you gone.' That was all he'd say about it, really. He took some of my hair and some blood with this weird thing that kind of looked like a thin silver gun. And I was like, 'What are you going to do with that?' And he said that it was insurance in case the race was exterminated, that maybe they could start us again and make us over in a nonviolent way. He said that they'd been studying us for centuries and that we had promise, but such great weakness, that we fought and glorified that violence while other parts of our consciousness deplored it. Still, he said, no species deserves to be extinguished and we'd already been so interfered with that he didn't think our little exchange would affect things that much. So, he was going to let me remember it, what happened. He made it sound like remembering it was rare and this great honor, thanks to my elevated intelligence or some such shit."

"That's nice of him, I guess," I say, thankful that I don't remember my own abduction, which happened when I was a baby. "It's nice to be told you're smart."

"He told me to try not to act out of fear, like when I went to shoot him. He said that all humans are afraid of death and we are violent because of that fear, but death was not something for humans to be afraid of." He shrugs. "That part *was* kind of nice, really."

"It sounds nice," I say because it does sound nice. Death hangs over all of us, looming there like the ultimate failure, but it would be cool to think of death in another way. Like if you think about it like this: Death isn't the absence of life, but the triumph over life. It's the end prize for having gone through life's turmoil and ups and downs. I'd like to think of it that way instead of the Big Badness that threatens us all. Obviously, my mother probably should have brought me to church.

"Deep thoughts, Mana?" China asks, shocking me out of my little thinking time.

"Naw. Never." I give them a blustery answer that's all rah-rah flippant. Wharff manages to grin back at me, which is really saying something about his level of awesome. Not everyone would get abducted by aliens and then manage to be nice to random people at a diner.

China asks him a couple of detailed questions about communication: if he could see the alien's eyes, if he saw other people on board the craft—human people—and whether or not those people looked like they were in trancelike states. Wharff repeats that the communication seemed to be telepathic, and says that he saw no other humans. He was in one small room with dull metal walls and no noticeable windows or doors, but it did sort of feel like other people were in there, too. There were crystals. I perk up at this, but a little muscle by China's eye twitches and I know that this is the information he's been waiting for.

I ask, "What kind of crystals?"

"Dark ones, like prisms." Wharff meets my eyes. "Why?"

"Just trying to imagine it. I'm into concrete details," I say without missing a beat, I don't think, even though the crystal moves a bit in my pocket.

"I'm like that as well. So, let's get this story over with. Don't you—"

"Did they say anything about how mankind was going to be obliterated?" China interrupts. "Any talk about machines? DNA?"

"No . . . not that I remember." Wharff clears his throat. "Yeah, so anyway . . . He cut a piece of my hair off. He told me that there was a war coming. A war that involved humans and aliens and that it was not likely the humans would win." He gulps. "I believed him. I don't know how humans could fight against things like him, with technology like they had. He sort of laughed and he said that it wasn't his type of alien that would be fighting with us. They were scientists, not warriors. Explorers, not fighters. So, I was like, then you're going to help us, right? And he said they didn't interfere with other cultures. Like *Star Trek*, you know? The prime directive that Captain Kirk was always breaking?" He lowers his voice, but his tone is still urgent. "It's messed up, honestly, because there is obviously already another alien race messing with us, so therefore they *should* interfere. I was getting angry then because I didn't think it was cool that they would just let us all die. And the alien guy held up the piece of hair he'd taken from me and said, 'We are preserving you. Your genetic material will ensure that your species will live on.' But not here? Not on Earth? I asked. He just sadly shook his head and then said, 'You never know the outcome of things, but it is not looking favorable.' I kind of lost it then, just started this crazy-ass angry weeping, and then he touched my face and I was back by my truck. Two hours had passed. My gun was on the passenger seat but the muzzle was melted so no bullets will ever come out of it again. What a waste of money. Guns are expensive."

A huge, wracking breath moves his chest in and out. He pushes both his palms flat on the table and scrutinizes us one at a time. "I know the story is whacked."

"It's not whacked," I say, thinking the only whacked part of it would be that there are only five kingdoms that are violent. "It's not whacked at all."

China grunts.

Wharff's chest does that strange heaving thing again and he excuses himself to go to the bathroom.

Once he's out of earshot China says, "Poor guy. Sucks when your concept of the world goes to pieces like that."

"Is he right?" I add some more salt to my french fries. "Is there going to be a war? A real war? Like in movies and stuff?"

China sighs. "Maybe. Possibly. If the machine gets assembled, they hardly need the bang-bang explosion kind of war."

"We need to stop that."

"Yes, we do."

"And get started on stopping it."

"Yep."

"China, you're not being Mr. Information here."

He brushes me off. "Sorry. Sorry. Soon."

I swallow hard. The french fries have all globbed into a big stone-shaped glob in my gut. At least that's what it feels like. "It's hard to be courageous with all of this stuff going on, you know?"

He accepts my topic change without even blinking. "Look, courage is something that has to be cultivated. The more often you are courageous, the easier it becomes. It isn't something that everyone is blessed with in abundance. You have it. Use it. The more you use it, the more courage sinks itself into your DNA and becomes synonymous with who you are," he says, and then I must have some sort of face because he goes, "What? Why are you looking at me like that?"

I try to sound tough and aloof. "Sometimes you're kind of deep, China." I pause and then a random thought comes into my brain. "Wait. Why is your nickname China? You aren't Chinese. Is that some sort of cultural appropriation?"

He makes a noise that sounds a lot like a guffaw. "No."

"What is it, then?"

He peers around the diner like he's more worried about someone overhearing this than Wharff's story. "When I was a little kid, really young, I had this tendency to fall off things and break. I fell off a couch, broke my arm, fell off a roof, broke my collarbone, fell—"

"You fell off a roof?"

"Yeah. Fell off a moving car, broke my leg. Fell off the diving board into the pool at the YMCA, broke my nose. So, my father, being the brilliant and loving jokester that he was, decided to call me China, not after the country but after the doll. You know? China dolls. They break easy."

"Wow. Douche move." I think about it for a second. "But isn't that still sort of wrong? Culturally? I mean, those dolls are made of porcelain."

"Exactly." He looks around toward the bathroom. "Wharff hasn't come out of there yet, huh?"

"Nope."

"He's been in there a long time."

"Some guys take forever to poop."

"Mana!" he scolds.

"What? You know they do."

He loses his jocular expression and gets a weird parental air about him, the kind my mom would get if I burped or something. I can't handle that. I don't need any surrogate parents, so I stand up. "I'm going to go check on him."

He stands up, too. "You're going to go into the men's bathroom and check on him?"

"Yeah."

"I don't believe that's legal."

"Whatever. You sound like Lyle." I pace away, darting between the tables, and throw over my shoulder, "I'll just knock."

If China responds to me, I don't hear it. Instead, I move past tables full of burgers and fries and the occasional salad, and make it to the restroom door. There's a symbol on it that's meant to represent a man. For a second, I hesitate. I don't know if this is a single-person bathroom or a stall situation. If it's stalls, Wharff might not even hear or notice if I knock.

"You think too much," I mutter.

And then I knock, loud and hard without apology, because that's the kind of person I am. I rap the door a good three times. There's no response.

Maybe it *is* a stall bathroom.

I reach for the doorknob and try to turn it. It's locked. Crap. Something like dread fills my chest. Who am I kidding? It is totally dread.

Knocking again, even louder, I call out, "Wharff? Mr. Wharff? You okay?"

There's no answer.

"Wharff? Hey! You okay in there?" My voice is now officially on the verge of panic.

The waitress comes over to me, looking concerned and slightly amused. Amused? "Everything okay?"

"Um . . . Ah . . ." I flounder. I'm not sure what to say and how to interact with her. This is because she has mostly been ignoring me. I am not sexy and giggle-inspiring.

China's suddenly right behind me. "Our friend is in there. He has blood sugar issues and sometimes passes out. The door locked, Mana?"

"Yeah." I am amazed at how smoothly he lies. No wonder I have trust issues.

"Oh! We have a key. You hold on just a minute." The waitress scurries off with a *poor dear* expression on her face. It is the face of pity. I hate that face. I've seen it a million trillion times since my mom went to the hospital. I reach out and knock again.

China tries the doorknob as if he has some sort of opening-doorknob magic mojo or something. It doesn't do anything different from when I tried.

"I could just break it open," he grumbles.

"I told you he was taking a long time."

"Are you seriously saying 'I told you so?'"

"Yeah."

"You are just like your mother. You're even unrepentant."

"Yeah." I let a smile move across my face despite my worry about Wharff. I used to never want to be compared to my mom, and yes, I am upset that she lied to me for years about who I am and what she does, but I still love her. It seems you can love someone even when you don't really trust them. "She does things because she believes in them. And she likes to be right. There's nothing wrong with that."

China rattles the doorknob and the waitress comes back, triumphantly dangling the keys in front of her. She has almost a sexy saunter as she appraises China. She slips in front of him and casts him a glance through her eyelashes. I almost vomit. There's a guy stuck in the bathroom and she's still trying to put the moves on China. Sighing isn't a good enough expression of my displeasure. I glance away and I swear I spot Wharff standing outside the window, beckoning me to join him. But it's a good distance away and the windows are so dirty that I'm not 100 percent sure it's him. I turn to grab China's arm and show him, but then I'm distracted by the waitress.

There's a little bit of a flirty flourish as she inserts the key into the lock and then turns the doorknob with a flick of her dainty wrist. She pushes the door in toward the restroom. The keys dangle there.

"Hel-lo?" Her voice is singsong, breaking one word into two melodious syllables. "Mist-er, you o-kay?"

The bathroom is completely empty and normal-looking—gray, boring, toilet paper clumped on the floor, paper towels hanging from a dispenser—but my breath hitches. It isn't right. Something isn't right. It smells, and not like a bathroom usually stinks. More like a gas station odor.

"China?" I step forward. "You smell that?"

He lifts his head, inhales, and swears in a quiet voice that I'm not used to him using. Fear fills my chest. Pivoting, he propels me out with his hand square on my back. His other hand yanks the waitress away from the bathroom door. She giggles. I swear to God. I gaze at where I thought I saw Wharff standing outside. Nobody is there.

"Out!" China yells the word like a cop. "Out! Everyone out! Now! Hurry!"

Almost all the diners start scurrying up and toward the front door without even asking why. China has that kind of commanding presence. Purses are hoisted onto shoulders. Coats are snatched but not put on. China smashes both doors open, but people are still slow moving through them, clustering and getting stuck.

"Mana! We need to get everyone out! Now!" China yells. I've never seen him so urgent and it is terrifying.

I give up hoping the people will be fast enough and grab a chair and swing it forward, breaking the giant windows next to the door. They are big and easy to step through. Someone, maybe a waitress, makes a protest noise, but other people help me move the jagged glass out of the way and then everyone hops through.

"Across the street! Go across the street!" China orders, moving people along. He plucks up an elderly woman who has a cane and sprints across the street with her, depositing her a good distance away. "Keep going!"

He starts back toward me and the waitress. We're trying to help a mom who has four kids and is limping. He hoists up the mom. This man has some serious muscles. He orders me, "Lift up the kids. Run!"

We do. I clutch twin boys, one on either side. Their pudgy hands instinctively cling to my back and arms and shoulders even though I'm a stranger. They trust me to take care of them. My stomach twists. I can't let them down, and I hurry even though I'm not sure what I'm hurrying from. Despite his heavier load, China has sprinted way ahead of us and already deposited the mom on the ground. Her sweatshirt heaves as she screams for her babies. The waitress lags slightly behind me. Then the air seems to shove us forward. I clutch the boys harder, refusing to let go, and twist because there is no way I'm not going to fall and if I'm going to fall, I'd rather not fall on my face. The air shoves me toward the buildings across from the restaurant, toward randomly parked cars, but I fight it and turn to face the diner.

That's when the sound comes, a bulky boom that rips through the streets like it's announcing a war. My mouth screams the word *no* but the sound is lost amid the screams and car alarms. I land on my back on the hood of a Ford F-150 truck. The boys stay in my arms, silent, but gulping in the burning air. For a moment, I can't register anything—what happened, where I am, why I'm holding blond-haired boys. Then China's face hovers above mine. He mouths my name, but I can't hear him. For a minute, my ears just don't work and the world is a weird silent nothing. Grabbing the boys from me, China says something again. The boys seem okay, just a little scraped and the one who has the name BILLY written on his bright blue sweatshirt starts to tear up, but he doesn't bawl.

China says something again, but it's like he's talking from a distance. Finally, I understand. He's asking, "Are you okay?"

I give him a thumbs-up even though I'm not sure what my mental or physical state is.

"You?" I yell back at him.

He gives me an *okay* sign. And then he jerks his thumb backward and rushes off. He's bending over people, helping them off the ground.

The waitress? Where is the waitress? Where are the other people? Sitting up slowly, I can finally get a full view of what's happening. The restaurant spews black and orange, smoke and flames. Parts of the building have landed on cars, including my mom's Subaru, which is half hidden under pieces of drywall and booths. People to the right and left are roaming around like zombies. Some have glass in their arms or bodies. The waitress is on the ground in front of me. The child she was holding is beneath her, screaming. I slide off the truck and go to them.

My hand reaches out before I can think about possible broken backs or necks, and I move the waitress sideways, rolling her off the child. The little girl keeps screaming. Her mouth is an open O, a gaping hole of anguish.

I try to cradle her in my arms.

"It's okay," I tell her, hunkering down. "It's okay. It's all over. You're okay."

But she just trembles against me and points over my shoulder. Every neuron inside of me is screaming not to look that way, that it's just the restaurant on fire, which is decidedly traumatic for anyone, especially a little kid.

Don't turn around, I think. *Don't look.*

I look.

And there above the restaurant, engulfed in smoke, is a metallic ship floating in the air. There are lights all along the bottom of it, and it is easily as big as the actual restaurant. This. This is what all of us are up against. This mammoth, technologically advanced thing. We are so little, so tiny beneath it.

To the right of the saucer and the diner, on the ground, is Wharff, I'm sure of it. He covers his mouth with one hand. With the other he gestures for me to come with him. Come with him? I shake my head.

"Come help!" I yell.

He gestures again and must realize I am really not coming. He turns and runs away, down the side alley and through the smoke.

The ship hovers there for a moment as we watch. Sirens scream their approach. Then a greenish gas explodes out the bottom of it. That must be why Wharff was covering his mouth. He knew the gas would come. He was trying to tell me. I slap my hand over the girl's mouth and order her, "Don't breathe! Hold your breath!"

CHAPTER 7

The bright green gas or vapor or whatever plummets out of the bottom of the ship. No holes are visible. It just billows down and out and into the air, coming toward us, flowing quickly, tumbling closer and closer.

"Hold your breath," I beg the little girl again. I'm not sure if she even hears me.

I point at the gas. I clamp my hand over my mouth and nose and then mime for her to do it, too.

She stops screaming and clamps her lips tight against one another.

I tuck her against my shoulder, hand still over her mouth and nose, and hold my own breath, too. The gas hits the people closest first, two men in flannel shirts that are part hipster and part lumberjack. They drop to the ground. Crap. A woman crumples. A child topples over. One by one, they fall.

And then the green gas wafts over the little girl and me like a wave of evil. The air gasps into something warm, but I refuse to inhale it. As the wave engulfs us, the UFO shoots straight up in the air and is gone in less than five seconds, completely disappearing into the sky, obscured by the heavy clouds.

It's like it was never there.

The gas passes us. Regular air returns, smoky and raw. Pulling the little girl away from my shoulder, I check out her eyes. They are open and wide and terrified. Mine probably are the same. But we are still standing. I whirl around as the gas hits other survivors. One after the other, they fall. They are helpless little dominos. We think our bodies are so strong, so tough, and then . . . We just topple.

Only China remains standing. He meets my eye but doesn't say anything. Then the gas is gone, just dissipated or something, and people start to stand up again. First it's the guys in flannel. They wander aimlessly around the sidewalk as fire trucks pull up, red lights swirling and alarms blaring. It's so tremendously loud.

And now the smoke that billows toward us is just regular smoke from the building. Burning plastic molecules sting our lungs. It smells horrible, but the air is breathable. The wind shifts again and the smoke blows up the street instead of across it. Firefighters pile out of ladder trucks and tankers. The one in control barks orders into his portable radio as others pull hoses off the trucks. They unravel into long, tan, snakelike things. One hose connects to the fire hydrant, others to a water truck. Through it all, people are aimlessly wandering around. Some bleed from explosion injuries.

The only one who seems dead is the waitress.

The waitress . . .

I hand the little girl to her mother and run back to the waitress to check on her. She still isn't moving. I start waving my arms above my head and yelling, "Here! This woman needs help over here!"

Two paramedics rush toward us, a man and a woman. The woman carries some sort of first aid kit. She feels for the waitress's pulse while the guy checks her eyes.

"She breathing?" I ask.

The woman nods. "Weak pulse. Shallow breaths. We need the stretcher."

The guy runs back to the ambulance.

"Should I help him?" I ask.

"You stay here. Tell me about the gas main. Is anyone still inside?" she asks.

"I don't think so," I say.

The little girl's mom comes over and starts checking out the waitress, sort of a mixture of concern and sobbing, and the girl goes, "What about the UFO?"

The paramedic cocks her head at me. "What?"

"The UFO. Above the restaurant," the girl says.

The male paramedic has returned, and he and the woman are now lifting the waitress onto the stretcher.

"Sweetie, I think you hit your head." Her mother makes big eyes at the paramedics.

The little girl pouts. "No . . . No, I didn't. I—"

"What do you remember?" I ask the girl's mom.

"I remember a fire alarm going off and us all evacuating the building. It blew up behind us, just a big fiery roar, right? Then the fire department arrived." Her mom cocks her head at me as if searching for approval and confirmation.

My mouth drops open. I realize it and shut it again. "You don't remember anything else?"

"Like what? Little green men?" She scoffs and puts her arm around her little girl's waist gently and protectively.

Her daughter stares up at her.

"How about we bring you to those nice ambulance people so you can get looked at," she says to the little girl, but she's also saying it to me.

I ask, "You don't remember the UFO, the green gas, any of that? Do you remember the big, brawny guy going into the bathroom? The waitress getting the keys?"

A man comes over and it's obvious he's been listening, too. He wraps an arm around my waist, just the way the woman did with the little girl.

"Let's go sit you down," he says.

His fingers tighten on my waist. He smells of grease and burgers and the smoke of the building. This poor man. Poor all of us. What have they done?

"I'm okay," I insist.

He doesn't believe me. "No. Sweetie, I really want you to go get checked out."

"I'm really okay, but thank you for caring and—"

China's voice interrupts my answer. "I'll take her over."

His arm slips around my waist, displacing the arm of the other man, who instantly lets go of me. When China goes into his in-charge mode, everyone steps in line. Except me. And Lyle. And maybe my mom.

"I'm okay," I insist even as China presses my side against his. "This is ridiculous!"

The man has switched his attentions to the little family. Firefighters rush by, shouting directions to one another. A couple more unroll a hose, hook it into the truck.

"Just play along with me." China's voice finds its way into my ear. "For once do not be difficult."

"I'm never difficult," I mutter, but he's kind of right. Whatever. I challenge anyone trying to deal with him on a long-term basis not to be quote-unquote difficult. However, I do play along with him, even pretending to limp as he steers me away from Mr. Worried Flannel Shirt Guy and toward the ambulances and paramedics. Doubt fills me. "You saw the UFO, right?"

"Of course. I held my breath, just like you. Good call there."

Oddly enough, I feel sort of proud. "So was that green stuff some kind of amnesia gas?"

He takes a sharp left away from the ambulances. "Exactly. The government often uses it to repress sightings and to avoid widespread panic."

I stop dead still. "The government? That was a flying saucer thing, China. It wasn't the government."

"No. It was. It was a military craft, actually. The U.S. military has about five of them. It was part of a trade program with one of the alien races."

I am not sure what I am supposed to think about this, and a sort of nauseated feeling spreads through me as I connect the dots. The government had control of that UFO. That means the government blew up the diner. *That* means the government hurt those people. Our government. Isn't our own government supposed to protect us? Keep us safe? No wonder my mom and China stopped working for them. And why? Why would the government hurt its own people? Why do they have those ships anyway? Or maybe I am completely jumping ahead in my thought process and it wasn't the government at all?

"A trade program? What did we trade?"

"Silence. Secrecy."

"About what? About them existing?"

"No. About the abductions."

Someone is yelling directions to someone else, words like *contain* and *safe* and *pressure,* so I'm assuming the shouter is a firefighter.

A cop comes running up, pauses when he reaches us, and says, "Are you two all right?"

"We're good," China answers.

The cop assesses us and then runs toward the fire. His run is military efficient. I envy that. I also envy his ignorance about what actually just happened. All the stuff I've witnessed swirls around in my head, the concepts and facts and faces clashing against each other in a confusing mess.

"Why would the government want to explode the diner? Wharff? Because he was there? Why would they care about him? There are a ton of abductees out there," I say, answering my own question. "Or was it just to keep it secret? But what secret? Nobody even would have thought of aliens until that saucer showed up."

"Maybe." China searches the area before moving us forward again. "We'll talk about it later, Mana Trent."

He used my full name. He never uses my full name. He must be serious.

"I want to talk about it now."

"Wharff might not have been the target."

"What do you mean?"

"I mean you might have been the target, or me." He keeps moving. "Wharff might have been the lure."

"But?"

"We need to focus on getting away right now, not on what happened." He shuts off all communication about this and I resent it.

We turn down another street, away from where my mom's car was parked. We can't get to it now. There's debris on it and the entire area is blocked off by emergency personnel. So, I ask, "How are we going to get home?"

"Walk."

"Walk?" I stutter the word out. "It's like three miles."

"Unless you want to call a friend."

I don't want to call Lyle or Seppie, not after what just happened at school.

"Okay. We walk. Wait, what about a taxi? Could we get a taxi?" I offer.

"That's lazy." He laughs. "Close your mouth, Mana. You're gaping at me."

I probably am. So I close my mouth for a second, breathe in, and will myself to be calm. "I know you don't want to talk about it, but please explain to me where Wharff went and what just happened, okay?"

"I don't know where Wharff went. We both saw him enter the bathroom. The door was locked from the inside. He was not there. What was in there instead was a bomb. The smell tipped me off. It's alien technology and well known to some of us. The most obvious scenario is that they were trying to cover up whatever happened to Wharff and keep him from telling us something important about his abduction."

"I thought I saw him outside, though."

"What?"

"Right before the explosion. It looked like he was beckoning me. And then after, right before the saucer came. I saw him cover his mouth and run away."

"You're sure it was him?"

"It was him or one of those shifter aliens."

For a second, China is silent. The world smells less of burning, but we, ourselves, reek. A woman asks us if we are okay and what happened, and China quickly tells her we are fine and there was an explosion at a diner. People pass by, checking on us, which is kind. Humans can be so kind.

Once they are gone I say, "Forgetting the confusion about Wharff, explain what you think happened next, okay?"

"Okay, once the building exploded, our government was alerted via sensors that send a high-alert transmission when that sort of explosion occurs. It senses the chemicals involved. They immediately dispatched the Northeast Saucer and tried to eradicate the memory of the event from everyone's brain."

"So, it wasn't the actual government that blew up the diner."

"It might have been, but I don't think so. I'm not a hundred percent sure. I don't exactly trust the United States government to deal with the alien threat, but blowing up a diner seems a bit extreme. Even for them."

This makes me feel a bit better, actually. But at the same time, I'm not cool with eradicating memories or not knowing what happened to Wharff. Then a phrase that China just used jars me.

"Wait. Northeast Saucer. Explain."

"It covers the eastern seaboard and interior New England from Virginia north."

"But people didn't forget the explosion. They forgot the gas and the saucer and Wharff."

"Exactly. That's the most telling part. They wanted us to forget

Wharff, too, which means that Wharff is important to the government or those aliens or both."

"But why?"

"That's the central question. Why?" He picks up his pace a little bit, but I keep up and he says, "I was meeting with him because we thought he might have some information, new information, on what the aliens were planning. Abductions are a dime a dozen. Some real. Some fake. The people in charge of the agency wanted me to meet with him, so I did. They told me to ask about crystals." He pauses. "Did your mother ever talk to you about aliens at all? Even as a fairy tale? Or a made-up story?"

"No." She talked to me about white chocolate–covered pretzels and grades and mom stuff. Not aliens. Never aliens. Never crystals, like the one in my pocket.

"Okay. Let's start at the beginning . . . the super-beginning." He coughs. "The ancient Sumerians . . ."

And my brain clouds over with memories of my world history fail earlier today. It seems like decades ago. How can so much even happen in one day after a month of nothing, of waiting?

"The ancient Sumerians . . . Are you listening?" he asks impatiently, and when I say I am, he continues, "They wrote on tablets three thousand years before the Bible. On those tablets the Sumerians detail exploits on other worlds, flying machines, huge battles on the Earth over the Earth."

"So what you're saying is that aliens have always been here?"

"Exactly. I'm saying there have always been aliens and for a while their presence was more obvious, much more obvious than now. The Nehilim, the Greek gods, the Starwalkers—so many names in so many cultures."

As we stride past the grocery store and the mini-mall attached to it, I try to imagine the Greek and Norse gods being actual living beings and not made-up fables. I wonder if Zeus was as randy as he was in the myths. I wonder if Odin really only had one eye.

But if they were real . . . "And then what? Why did they stop coming?"

"To understand that, we have to understand what humans are."

His pause is so long that I have to ask, "Which is?"

He swallows hard. I watch his Adam's apple move in his neck. "Prototypes. We were seeded here. These protohumans were initially four feet tall and super-hairy. They were planted and then the aliens left. A lot of abductees have been told this same story."

"But why just plant us and leave?"

"Who knows? An experiment, maybe? Just to see how we evolve?" He puts on his sunglasses even though we are not facing the sun as we walk. "*The Book of Enoch* says, 'Go tell the Watchers of heaven, who have deserted the lofty sky, and their holy everlasting station, who have been polluted with women. And have done as the sons of men do, by taking to themselves wives, and who have been greatly corrupted on the earth . . .'"

"So these four-feet tall, hairy Earth women are so sexy that the aliens had to go?" I raise an eyebrow.

"Sort of."

"What is this *Book of Enoch*?"

"It's ancient, a Jewish religious piece. There are sections that date from 300 B.C. But it's not part of the biblical canon. Most people don't consider it inspired by God or anything like that. Well, the Ethiopian Orthodox Tewahedo Church does, as does the Eritrean Orthodox Tewahedo Church, but that's it."

I stop really paying attention.

"It's believed Enoch wrote it before the big flood—the Noah's ark flood."

I have no idea who Enoch is, but I'm not liking this whole concept. "Everyone is always blaming women and sex. I hate that."

"It's hate-worthy," China agrees. "Basically, the book says that evil is here because fallen angels are here. The fallen angels are here to procreate with human women."

"So all evil is human females' fault?" I scoff. "Nice. I bet men wrote that."

"The book reads, 'And they became pregnant, and they bore great giants, whose height was three hundred ells. Who consumed all the acquisitions of men. And when men could no longer sustain them, the giants turned against them and devoured mankind,' but not all of mankind, obviously, because some still existed. And the fallen angels began 'to sin against birds, and beasts, and reptiles, and fish, and to devour one another's flesh, and drink the blood,'" he says as I shudder.

I don't want any of that to be true. "But what about the aliens you talk to? Aliens like Pierce? What do they say? Are they the implanting aliens who have come back?"

"No. None are. Pierce's people blended into the Earth after their own planet was attacked by another race. They became the Fae— the pixies and elves and fairies of folklore. The Wendigos and that troll-like alien that attacked you in the bathroom this morning are pretty much enslaved by the Samyaza here. Those are the ones you have to worry about."

"The ones that want to get rid of all the humans." I stop walking for a second. The sounds of the diner and the sirens are far behind us. The destruction was small but immense. If they can do that, what else can they do?

China stops with me. "Yes."

"Why?"

"Why what?"

"Why do they want to get rid of us?" I wipe at my lips with the back of my hand. They are so dry that they feel crusty.

"We are just too many. A swarm of bugs to them, semi-clever bugs. We'd never give up our Earth to them. So they need to get rid of us so they can have the planet." He says it all so matter-of-factly.

Bugs.

Inconsequential.

Experimented on.

Abducted.

Bugs.

What would that make me? A super-bug?

I blink away the memory of the explosion, the waitress, unmoving on the ground. "Why don't they just vaporize us or something? Like an ant bomb. Just be done with us?"

"They'd miss some of us. Some would hide in bunkers or rural Maine or Louisiana or Tibet or wherever. They need a precise technology to eradicate all of us without having to hunt every single one of us down and without harming the Earth's actual atmosphere, which is a bit of a paradise to them."

"And this precise technology?"

"Involves isolating DNA, obviously. It has to be DNA that only occurs in humans and not other alien species or animals—that's harder than you imagine—and, using that, creating a biological agent to spread the poison by having it only attracted to that DNA . . . and then creating the machine itself to spread it. Or at least, that's what we think. We could be wrong." He steps over a pile of dirty old snow that has accumulated in the breakdown lane and hasn't yet been melted by sun, like most of the other snow. "I'm sorry. This is a lot of information to dump on you."

"I'd rather just know, just get it out in the open." I pause to kick the snowbank with my yellow Keds, suddenly glad that I didn't dress up for school today. "Why do they have to assemble the machine anyway? Like, why aren't the parts all put together already?"

China keeps walking forward. His leather jacket stretches across his shoulder blades. Smoke has smudged a spot ashen. A tiny rip mars the fabric at the bottom of his jacket. My clothes haven't fared better from that explosion. I trot after him because he hasn't broken his pace at all. The man is a robot, I swear. "China?"

"It's a good question. I think the machine takes time to assemble and they worried about people like us being able to eradicate centuries' worth of work if we located the machine prior to its implementation. So it has been assembled in secret in steps in a location we are still trying to determine. But now . . . well, the latest intelligence is saying that it's all a ruse. That the machine is already assembled. That it isn't a machine at all. It's just waiting to be activated."

"You don't know where?"

"No." He sighs. "This is all conjecture. We don't know anything for certain. I mean, we call it a machine, but all we really know about it is that it involves crystals and chips."

Crystals. Like the one in my pocket.

"And how close are they to being done building it?"

"Our sources say really close. But again, none of the information is solid."

"But your sources don't say where. Or what it looks like?"

"No."

"Lovely."

A short burst of laughter erupts out of his mouth, and it seems involuntary. "Exactly. Lovely." He stops. Touches his coat pocket. "Damn it, I lost my phone."

As we walk, I search for *The Book of Enoch* on my phone's Web surfer application. Some of the fallen angels taught humans, I guess. Because the text I find reads:

And Azâzêl taught men to make swords, and knives, and shields, and breastplates, and made known to them the metals of the earth and the art of working them, and bracelets, and ornaments, and the use of antimony, and the beautifying of the eyelids, and all kinds of costly stones, and all coloring tinctures. And there arose much godlessness, and they committed fornication, and they were led astray, and became corrupt in all their ways. Semjâzâ taught enchantments, and root-cuttings, Armârôs the resolving of enchantments, Barâqîjâl, taught astrology, Kôkabêl the constellations, Ezêqêêl the knowledge of the clouds, Araqiêl the signs of the earth, Shamsiêl the signs of the sun, and Sariêl the course of the moon.'

We're almost at the two-mile mark when I ask China, "Do you think *The Book of Enoch* is real?"

He shrugs. "What's real, honestly?"

"Don't get all philosophical-stoner on me," I tell him, slightly miffed that he won't give me a straight answer.

A huge white dog runs by. Its leash drags behind after it. It's the same dog I saw at school earlier. There have been a lot of dogs barking in the distance today. It couldn't have all been this one, could it? Lunging, I grab the end of the red leash. Sailboats decorate it. The dog stops abruptly, turns, and stares up at me with big, sweet brown eyes.

"I don't see its owner," I say.

China spins around, searching. "Me either."

He squats down and reaches between all the messy fur to read a tag. "It has a number."

"Call it," I insist, scruffing up the dog's fur behind her ears. I think it's a her.

China asks for my phone. I explain that his phone actually wasn't in his coat pocket but is hanging out of his pants pocket. The dog licks his face and he laughs. China actually laughs. I almost fall over from shock and try to imagine him in a different life, a normal life. What would he even be? In the Marines? A cop? A football quarterback? A top chef? I can't even imagine. But he would definitely be someone with a dog.

"It's a recording," he whispers as his free hand pets the dog's furry head. His face hardens.

"They're dead."

"What?"

"The dog owner is dead." He hangs up and calls again so that I can hear the message, which is a woman's voice, breaking, saying that her grandma and grandpa have died and to please send donations to the American Society for the Protection of Animals. The message box is full so we can't leave a message.

I stare into the dog's eyes. How long has the poor thing been wandering around? "Then who do we bring her to?"

"The pound."

"No way," I say. "We are not abandoning her to the pound. What if it's a kill shelter? No way."

I hug the dog to my chest. She lets me. She rests the bottom of her big muzzle on my shoulder. Her breath is, to put it gently, a bit like eggy tuna, but I don't care.

China's face softens.

"We can't take her to a pound," I say.

"She's a dog, Mana. She's a responsibility. As much as I love dogs—"

"I need her," I interrupt. "I don't have anyone I can trust."

There. I said it.

"Trust is . . . It's a liability in this job, but it makes you whole, Mana." He pets the dog's back in long sweeping gestures. Tiny bits of fur flutter up in the air. She's shedding.

"You don't trust anyone," I sputter. The dog licks my cheek.

His hand stops stroking the dog's back. "I trusted your mother."

I don't know what to say to that, honestly, so I just keep stroking the dog's back.

"You trust Seppie," he says after a moment.

"Usually." I cringe. "But I don't want to make her life any harder with all this stuff, you know? Lyle—Lyle's already involved."

"She's involved just by knowing," China says. He picks a tiny piece of dried-up leaf out of the dog's fur.

"I don't want her to be the kind of involved where she misses school and loses her chance to get into a good college and have the kind of happy life she wants."

"There's a chance that there will soon be no college," he says. "No kids taking their SATs or AP tests."

"I am not sure that's so bad," I half kid. "I mean, annihilation of humankind is bad, but no more standardized tests judging your aptitude and determining your future as part of a commercialized venture to make those testing companies money? That sounds pretty good to me."

His gaze meets mine. The dog licks my chin.

"I still don't understand why you think you aren't smart," he says.

"I don't test well." I give a shrug like it doesn't matter, but it does. It's hard having teachers think you're dumb. It's hard not doing as well at school as your two best friends—one best friend now, I guess, since Lyle freaked out in the bathroom.

"You talk about not trusting people? I talk about not trusting tests." He gives a little snicker. "Although to be fair, tests are made by people . . ."

"So if you don't trust tests, you don't trust people, since they are the ones who made the tests? Is that what you're saying?"

He grabs the dog's leash. "Exactly. Now, what should we name this beast?"

"Do we get to keep her?"

Nodding, he passes the leash to me as I stand up. I launch myself into a hug, wrapping my arms around him. It's a bit like hugging a tree. The dog wags her tail and yips.

"You should name her," China says.

"She probably already had a name."

"We'll never know it."

I think about it as we start walking again and I finally say, "Enoch."

"That's a guy's name."

I try to express my displeasure at his limited scope with a grunt.

He raises his hands up in the air like he's surrendering. "I get it. I get it." After a moment he adds, "But do you know who Enoch was? Or is it just because we were talking about the book?"

"The book," I admit. "Plus, she seems like an Enoch."

Enoch stops to pee on a utility pole. I glance away because it seems rude to watch. China taunts me about my "tender sensibilities," but I don't rise to his bait. I'm too tired out to debate or taunt back. Teasing takes energy.

Once we start walking again, China says, "Enoch was one of the ten pre-deluge patriarchs. The deluge being the flood—the biblical Noah's ark flood. You do know what that was about, right?"

"Of course," I say, but he still explains that Noah's flood was actually an attempt to destroy mankind. Noah survived because he was warned. The flood story isn't just Christian, but also can be found in Greek mythology, in India's Puranas, in the Mayan history of the K'iche' people, as well as in that of the Lac Courte Oreilles Ojibwas of Wisconsin. He rattles all this off with more confidence than my world history teacher.

"The deluge," he announces, "was allegedly the aliens first attempt to get rid of us humans."

I stop walking.

"In the Babylonian account of the flood, the Hindu narrative, and the book of Genesis, a man is told that the flood is coming and warned to build a vessel to keep him and his family safe. "He lets out a sigh. "It's commonly believed that Pierce's race saved them, warned them. Some say it was God. That works, too. I don't know."

"So, why don't they just do that again? Why build a machine?"

"It obviously didn't work well last time." He waves an arm to show the proliferation of human civilization all around us. "Plus, it's a geological nightmare. That wasn't my point, though. I wanted to tell you what Enoch means."

"Okay."

"It means 'he who does not see death,' and it says in Genesis that 'he was not; for God took him.'"

"You mean, Enoch just sort of left the Earth."

"Basically. He was taken to heaven and became the head archangel, guardian of all of heaven's treasures. And he is the angel that communicates God's words to everyone else."

"Wow. That's kind of a promotion."

He laughs. "You can say that again."

"Wow. That's kind of a promotion."

"I didn't mean it literally!" He whines to Enoch the Dog that I am silly and much too literal, but I know he secretly thinks I'm funny. I spend the rest of our walk thinking about floods, and gas, the waitress, the poor dead alien in the bathroom, Lyle, my mom, Wharff and how his horrible experience makes me feel not so alone—all these random things that I shouldn't have to think about. Not once do I think about my history test.

CHAPTER 8

e remember that we've actually left China's car at the hospital, so we end up walking two and a half miles to the hospital instead of three toward home, which shouldn't seem as much of an awesome event as it feels. It's been that kind of day, the kind of day where you see death and aliens and green amnesia gas and flying saucers controlled by your own government. It is the kind of day when your own best friend breaks up with you because he can't take how weird your life has gotten even though his own life is totally weird. But at least it is also the kind of day where you get a dog.

As we reach China's Jeep, he asks, "Lyle hasn't tried to call you? Or text?"

"Nope."

"That doesn't sound like him."

"Dumping me because of all this doesn't sound like him either."

"You drive." China clicks his seatbelt into lock position and I back out of the parking space. "You're sure it's him?"

"Of course I'm sure," I lie, but now that he's asked I realize that I'm not actually sure at all.

And then Enoch starts growling from the backseat. The car smells intensely of dog.

My ears perk up. "What is it, baby?"

China scowls.

And there is Seppie fast-walking at us. Seppie! Joy leaps into my face and I can't stop smiling. Lyle's right next to her. I thought she was going to camp and Lyle was . . . My brain tries to understand what's happening, but I can't. They have crowbars in their hands like they are construction workers.

"What are they doing?" I ask, trying to figure it all out. Seppie is not a crowbar type of person.

"Move, Mana." China's voice is a hard thin thing.

"What?"

"Go!" He leans over and blares the horn—a loud horrible noise. Enoch starts barking, but Seppie and Lyle? They don't respond at all. No jumping. No yelling. No smiling. If anything, their walk becomes more focused, harder, faster.

"What's wrong with them?" I do not accelerate. I sit there in the car, motionless, staring at Seppie and Lyle. Rigidity distorts their normally happy faces. Seppie's hair is not perfect. Lyle's shirt is tucked in. I am suddenly cold and horrified. "Something is seriously wrong with them."

"Go! I'll explain," China insists.

"I'm not. I'm not going. They're my friends; I have to take care of them." Before he can say anything, I open the door and leap out of the Jeep.

His voice is a growl of anger and outrage, but I ignore it and rush toward them. Enoch barrels after me, barking and growling even louder.

I yank her back by her leash. "No, baby . . . no . . ."

And in all that hectic wildness, I sort of lose track of what's going on for a second. When I look back up again, China has jumped into the driver's seat, which is not adjusted for him, and his legs are folded up and he's yelling, "Get in the car! Get back in the car right now, Mana!"

But Enoch is barking so loudly and straining, trying to get to Seppie and Lyle, that I can't even imagine trying to get in the car again.

"Lyle!" I yell. "Seppie! You guys okay?"

And that's when Lyle screams, dropping the crowbar. This makes no sense. Is he okay? What is going on? He grabs at his head like he has the mother of all migraines and I want to take care of him, but something holds me back. Fear? Seppie runs at me, silent. She lifts the crowbar like a weapon—like a weapon that she's going to use against me.

"No!" I duck and she misses. She tried to hit me! "Seppie!"

Enoch leaps for Seppie's arm and latches on. Her doggy teeth grab at Seppie's bulky parka that Seppie always thinks makes her look too rugged, but her parents insist that she wear because it has a negative-fifteen-degrees cold rating.

Seppie's crowbar drops to the asphalt.

"I have to get you," she says. "I have to get you!"

And her voice is a plea and a cry. But then there's Lyle and he's picked up the crowbar and he's waving it in front of my face.

"Mana, we have to get you," he says, and his voice is not right either.

"Lyle?" My own voice breaks when I say his name. Fear ripples through me. Something is terribly wrong with him. "Are you guys okay?"

Enoch lets go of Seppie and growls, standing in front of me, guarding me from both of my best friends. Her fur stands up straight. Her ears flatten against her skull. Seppie's coat is ripped, but it doesn't look like she's bleeding.

"Guys . . . what are you talking about?" I ask.

China's hand grabs me and he's shoving me into the backseat of the Jeep before I realize what's happening. Slamming shut the door, he ignores my protest and spins around to confront Seppie and Lyle. But they are lunging at the car, trying to open my door and get to me.

"Dog!" he yells and Enoch leaps into the front passenger seat. China rushes into the driver's seat and slams the door, locking it.

Seppie and Lyle bang at the window like zombie extras on an AMC prime-time show.

"What is going on?" I pant out the words, scrambling to get away from the window, which Seppie is trying to break with the crowbar. China accelerates and the car lurches forward. The crowbar slams into metal between the windows. Enoch falls off the front seat with a yelp. I manage to pull myself through the space between the bucket seats and get shotgun. Enoch clambers onto my lap. I throw my arms around her so she won't fall again.

"Get your seatbelt on," China orders.

"I can't, she's in the way."

"Get your seatbelt on now!"

"Why?"

"They're coming."

"Who? Seppie and Lyle?" Not even Lyle can run that fast.

"Not Seppie and Lyle," he says, jerking his thumb backward. "Everyone."

Craning my head, I peek behind us. There are people—people everywhere—filling the street. Grandmothers, children, police officers, firefighters, hospital workers. There are people in wheelchairs, people without their coats on and just in hospital gowns. There are people of all different races, but they are mostly white because New Hampshire is demographically mostly white—95 percent, I memorized that. Asians? 2 percent. There are people of all different ages, but they're mostly over forty, probably because we're by the hospital. The only thing that they all have in common is the expression on their faces—steely-eyed, determined, mouths open and demanding—and their movement. They are all rushing forward, toward us, toward the car.

"China?" My voice is a squeak.

"Hold on, Mana."

I turn to face the front and manage to finally get my seatbelt on despite my shaking hands and Enoch's 125-pound presence on my lap. I grab her again. She doesn't seem safe. None of us seems safe.

"What is going on? Why are they chasing us?"

"You. They are chasing you. That's what Lyle said. He was 'getting' you."

"Why are they getting me?"

"Don't get hysterical."

"I am *not* hysterical and *you* are *not* helping."

"I'm trying to get us out of here." He veers around two people wearing bright pink hospital volunteer vests and carrying electrical cords. "What the—"

One of them throws herself on the hood of the car and rolls off. Enoch snarls.

"What is happening?" I demand.

China's silent for a second. "Mind control. I can't think of anything else."

Mind control? I look back again. So many. There are so many. Some of them are barefoot. Except—

"But you're fine. Why are you fine?" I stare at China as he speeds out of the parking lot finally. We careen down the access road to the hospital, past the man-made water retention pond and the hospital's generators.

"Not a good time to talk about this." He frantically turns the wheel of the car to the right to avoid a police officer who is setting up a spike mat across the roadway.

"It's a pursuit termination device," he says. "Damn it."

If we hit that, our tires will flatten instantly and China will lose control of the Jeep.

Instead, he loses control of the Jeep anyway, up on the sidewalk, zigzagging one way and then another. He hits a garbage can.

"That's going to dent," I say quietly.

He growls again. Enoch leaps into the backseat.

"I'm just saying. Do you own this Jeep or does my mom?"

"When your mother wakes up, a little dent is going to be the least of her worries."

This is most likely true, but Mom is one of those people who hates anything ruining the perfection of her car, even if it is a Subaru. It already had the giant dent from the Wendigo. And then the event at the diner pretty much decimated it.

China gets the Jeep back onto the roadway, safely beyond the police officer. The people here act . . . normal—just walking, not really looking at us. Going about their happy people business.

"Is that it?" I ask.

"I think so."

"Are all those people back at the hospital . . . are Seppie and Lyle still . . ." I struggle for the words because the words are too weird to utter. "Mind controlled?"

"It wears off. Thankfully."

We go up on the highway, taking the ramp quickly. It's just four and the sun is beginning to set, bringing down the cold, scary night sky. The snow is here now. The sky can't give us any more warnings about what might come; no matter how hard I stare at it, I won't see stars through the darkness.

China clears his throat next to me. His eyes squint like he might be needing glasses to drive at night. His grip on the steering wheel loosens and is no longer white-knuckled. Enoch sits in the backseat, perfectly content.

I shift my gaze to the front window, then think better of it, pulling up my yellow Keds so that I can retie them. I should get the kind without laces. Someday something as simple as an unlaced shoe might be the end of me. I try to slow my breath down, bring calmness into my heart, but I'm barely handling this.

Almost like he reads my thoughts, China says, "It's okay to occasionally let it get to you."

"I'm trying to be better than that now," I respond, tightening the knot as I reference the time before. The last big amount of time we were together, when my mom was missing, I had multiple freak-out moments when I realized aliens were real, that some were super-dangerous, that I was not normal, that my mom was kidnapped. It was not one of the shiniest times in the history of Mana. My heart twists; at least back then Lyle cared. "Explain to me about the mind control. Why are they coming after me?"

"You must have something someone wants."

The crystal. It has to be the crystal.

"Something *who* wants?" I ask.

He lifts a shoulder like he doesn't know.

"It appears shoulders can lie."

"What?" He sniffs in like he has a cold.

"You're pretending with this nonverbal action like you don't know who is mind-controlling everyone. But you always answer with words. Therefore, your shoulder is lying."

Enoch barks, which I take as agreement. Reaching back, I show her my hand. She slaps it with her paw, giving me five.

"I need to be able to trust you, China," I say after he doesn't answer for a good thirty seconds. "I'm not even sure where we're going."

"I've told you not to trust anyone," he grumbles.

"I'm doing a good job at that," I admit, and even as I admit it, I know that it's hard. I don't like this world where there is nobody I can depend on. I don't like this world in which I can't just know what the hell is going on and where people's hearts and intentions are. Lyle. Seppie. They tried to kidnap me.

It's almost like he's reading my mind again because he says, "It wasn't them. They weren't controlling their actions."

"Whatever."

"You could see Lyle fighting it. He threw that crowbar down and grabbed his head in pain. He was trying, which is remarkable. Truly. You can't blame them when they are under cognitive intervention and control."

"*You* aren't."

He shrugs. The sky darkens even more. Car headlights switch on. Taillights resemble eyes, sinister eyes. I tilt my head back against the seat's headrest. It's too high, though. Enoch circles and resettles in the backseat.

"Are you going to tell me why you weren't?" I ask.

China sighs. "When . . . when I joined the government, there were some . . . procedures that they did. It was to prevent this sort of thing from happening."

"Procedures?"

"Just a tiny bit of brain surgery. No big deal."

I gasp and he laughs. "Aren't you going to ask me the important question?"

"The important question?"

"Yeah."

"Which is . . . ?"

"Well, that's a decent one, 'which is,' but I meant, 'China, how about why wasn't *I* mind-controlled? Wouldn't it have been more effective and efficient to just control me?' Or maybe, 'Who is doing this?' "

"I asked the last one! You just didn't answer." I would pout, but that seems childish. So, instead, I focus on tying my other shoe. Today was the kind of day where running is important and tonight seems like it's not going to be much better.

I wait.

He drives. He puts on the radio instead of answering. It's a report about the Side Street Café exploding.

"Investigators say a faulty gas main is likely to blame in an explosion that destroyed a local diner and took the life of a—"

I click it off.

He puts it on again.

I turn the volume down.

Enoch puts her head down on her paws and instantly begins snoring.

I wait some more. And finally I lose my patience. "Listen, if you want me to trust you, you need to at least answer my questions."

"*Listen*, you already do trust me whether you admit it or not," he says, mimicking my use of the word *listen*, which I use too much, admittedly. "And you need to actually ask me the questions."

"I did! I asked you before. I asked at least one of them." I take a deep breath. "This is a ridiculous thing to bicker about. I'm going to ask the questions. One. Are Seppie and Lyle okay? Two. Why am I not mind-controlled? Three. Who is doing this?"

"I don't know if your friends are okay. I'm assuming that they are."

My heart twists. "They have to be okay. We should—we should go back."

"We both know they are long gone from there. Once they are no longer under the influence, they'll go back to what they were doing before. If they stay under someone's control, they'll be looking for you."

I exhale. He's probably right, but I still feel like I've abandoned them even though they were technically attacking me. My body buzzes from the tension and adrenaline. Horrible. There is nothing more horrible than seeing your friends taken away from you, their minds and actions distorted. They were not themselves, I try to convince myself. They were not Lyle and Seppie.

"Life is not easy," I announce.

"True. Second question," China continues. He is not the sort of person who dwells in the Land of Self-Pity. I try to respect this, but sometimes a little self-pity is sort of therapeutic. "I have no certainty about why you aren't mind-controlled but I'm assuming it is for the same reason that I'm not. Someone made sure that you couldn't be. If that was your mom, the government, the aliens who abducted you? I have no clue. Question number three. Who is doing this? That's a good one. Question number four is even better. That is *why*."

"Sometimes you sound like a teacher—the bad kind of teacher—and you've already told me why: I have something they want or

I *am* something they want or whatever," I grumble, because even though this is interesting and important stuff, China is not my teacher or my parent and sometimes when he does these information dumps, I feel like he's talking down to me, which could be—to be fair—my own insecurity, or it might just be that he actually *is* talking down to me. My adrenaline is too jacked up right now to do any real deep soul searching about this, and to be honest, I'm not sure the development of my self-awareness should be my primary focus when the excrement has just hit the fan, excuse my French, as Mom and Wharff would say.

China does not respond to my teacher insult. Instead, he just clears his throat and keeps talking. "I'm assuming that they are trying to get you because they perceive you as a threat or a potential ally. Or you have what they want."

Sometimes, I swear, he just likes to hear himself talk.

"And who is *they*?" I study his profile as he drives through the night. My words are hard and tough and match how I feel inside. Hard. Tough. Walled off. Detached from this. But I'm *not* detached, because *this* is about me. Someone is trying to get me. This isn't about just the crystal. This isn't about just my friends' betrayal. This is specific to me because of who and what I am and what is in my pocket. This is a big-picture sort of thing.

He swallows hard. "I'd rather not tell you."

"Seriously?"

He gives a bit of a shrug. "You already have enough trust issues, Mana."

"You're the one who told me not to trust!"

"Exasperation does not become you."

"Well, then, don't be a dick."

"Fine. It's Pierce," he says, turning in to a driveway or maybe a dirt road. The headlights illuminate trees as the car rumbles over the uneven surface. "The only one I know who is powerful enough to do that much mind control is Pierce."

CHAPTER 9

He stops the car in the middle of the darkness, turns it off, and waits. He knows me well enough by now to know that I'm going to have questions.

"Pierce?" I unbuckle my seatbelt. All I can see in front of me is woods, woods, and more woods. "You are saying that Pierce just mind-controlled all those people in an attempt to get me? You are saying that Pierce isn't actually dead?"

"Possibly and yes."

He unbuckles his seatbelt as well while I attempt to wrap my head around the newest development. Pierce is Fae, an alien species that people explain away as fairies or pixies or magical folk, only they're not little. Pierce, specifically, is beautiful and sort of sparkly (an embarrassing trait, I imagine, because of the whole *Twilight* thing with vampires) and she used to work with my mom and China. Lyle and I met her when everything went wrong last year. She noticed that I could hear aliens' thoughts sometimes. That was because I could hear some of hers. Some. Not all. When my former crush/evil alien Dakota attacked us, we assumed Pierce had died. But when I used the crystal, it looked like Pierce was there in the background . . . but the Australian guy called her Fey, didn't he? To be fair, I want so badly for Pierce to be alive that I could probably delude myself into thinking that was her, but I also want her to be a good guy, not a bad guy.

Truth is, I want everyone to be good guys and sometimes I feel like there are no good guys at all.

"Where are we?" I ask after we open the doors and stand outside of the car. The world is quiet, almost too quiet. No little forest animals are scurrying anywhere.

China's voice suddenly shouts out, "Mana, duck!"

I dive down to the snow even as I hear the telltale "Exterminate."

The Wendigo lands right where I was standing. Its gaunt, emaciated body gives it an undead guise and hides how strong and dangerous it is. Its skin is ashy gray and the thing smells so bad—like decay and old garbage and mold—that it makes me gag.

"Exterminate." The mouth is full of scissor-sharp teeth. Its black eyes focus on me.

"China . . . ?" He must have an appropriate weapon for this.

Enoch's snarling body leaps into the air even as I scream for her to stay back. She snatches the Wendigo by its head and rips it off. By the time all four of her dog paws are back on the ground, she's spat the head back out. It rolls, lifeless, across the snow.

I yank her toward me, hugging her doggy body to my chest. "Enoch! You could be hurt!"

She licks my face. Her tongue smells like blood. I try not to think about this and just bury my head in her fur for a second.

China's voice comes from above us. "That is not a normal dog."

"She's special," I say.

He makes some sort of sputtering sound. "Yeah, she's special, all right."

I just hug her more tightly for a second and then whisper, "Thank you for saving us."

She tries to lick me again, but I stand up, brushing snow off my pants. I stay close to her as I stare up at China and wonder if there are any more Wendigos hanging about waiting to attack. Enoch seems calm, though. After a moment I ask China where we are exactly, other than a Wendigo attack center. I am only half kidding.

"Big-time headquarters," he says, pressing a button on the screen of his cell phone. A tree splits in half, revealing the bright, steel sides of an elevator.

"Did you kill a tree to do this? Or is this a fake tree?" I ask after my moment of shock passes. I grab my bag, which still has the crystal in it, and hit my thigh to get Enoch to come.

"You care about the tree?"

"Of course." I almost scoff because who wouldn't care about a tree, but decide against it and instead just stride toward the elevator tree, trying not to worry about things lurking nearby. Lyle would love this.

But before I can get there, China stops me with a hand on my arm. "Mana."

His face is illuminated only by the moon and the stars. It looks . . . worried.

"I haven't been telling you something."

My breath escapes me. "Join the club."

He doesn't move away, I'll give him that. When China shares difficult information he doesn't shirk or make excuses or hide or distance himself, he just says it (eventually), and I appreciate that bit of bravery and forthrightness. Enoch relieves herself on a tree that is not an elevator and prances back toward me, pressing her side into my shins and knees like she's either blocking me from moving forward, creating a protective doggy barricade between me and China, or else just looking for some love. I scratch her ears in case it's the third option and say, finally, "Okay. What is it?"

We're facing each other and I have to gaze up a bit, but then he spreads his feet a little, shortening himself. He checks a text on his phone and clears his throat.

"I'm just going to get this out. Do you know how I asked you if you wanted to help me with this—?" He waves a hand to indicate the sky above us, the world around us, all dark and obscured, and then continues, "Well, it turns out that wasn't up to me."

"What do you mean?" I duck my head and focus on Enoch because the pity in China's usually pitiless eyes is too much for me.

"I mean, there are people higher up than I am in the organization—"

"I thought this was a renegade organization."

"It is, but we still have a hierarchy." He puts a heavy hand under my chin and lifts my head up to look at him. "They think you are too much of a risk to use. That's why—that's why there's been so much silence on my part. I never should have offered to let you help. I believe you can absolutely be vital to our mission. I'm—"

But the world has stopped. Anger rolls up into my throat, hot and full of acid.

"A risk?" I interrupt. "What the hell do you mean? How am I a freaking risk?"

He doesn't even hesitate. "They think you're an unknown, Mana. You're human with alien tweaks. You've been messed with. They don't know if you have some brainwashing element still underlying all your external persona. They don't—"

I swear.

He stops talking.

"Pierce can't brainwash me. You just said that. I highly doubt I have some freaking subliminal programming underneath it all. What do they think? I'm just going to go crazy and blow up the world?"

He doesn't answer.

"Seriously?" I give up. This is just stupidity. I stride toward the tree.

"Mana!"

I shake my head and keep walking.

"The aliens made a treaty with Eisenhower in the 1950s, the ones people call the Grays, working with the Samyaza."

The tree shines like a freaking beacon in the darkness, illuminated from within. Enoch keeps pace with me, leaning against my legs, her shoulder lightly grazing me, and I keep my left arm down so that my fingers can feel the soft fur of her back.

I stop and turn back to him, standing there in the darkness and cold. The night sky is thick above us. You'd think it would make me feel safer, the darkness. It doesn't. "What are you saying?"

He moves forward three or four strides, closing the distance between us. "They made a deal—the United States government and the Grays, the Samyaza."

"Yes, we know this. They said they could abduct people for technology or something. I'm cold. Can we not do this now?"

"They duped the government. They said that their planet was dying, that their species was dying. They needed humans to help strengthen their own DNA, to help their species survive. They appealed to our humanity." His laugh is short, bitter, and it catches me off guard. Enoch presses against my legs as China continues, "We gave them underground bunkers. We gave them permission as long as they promised that no humans would be harmed; that the abductions would be limited; that the humans, the abductees, would have no memory of what happened. They broke the promises. They took enzymes. They took blood. They experimented, genetic experiments that would make the Nazi doctors of World War Two envious. Survivors call one of the levels at a bunker 'Nightmare Hall.'"

I shudder. I don't want to hear this. Panic starts to rise inside of me. "Why are you telling me this?"

"You need to know how serious this is, Mana. How big." He comes and grabs my hand in his, engulfing it. I let him. "They crave us. They crave our blood, our DNA, our enzymes. Many abductees become food, strung up and used. Some get implants—implants that could potentially control them when the Grays and Samyaza decide they need to be controlled."

"To do what?"

"An army. A human army to fight alongside them when they decide to take over the world."

The woods are silent.

"That's not going to happen," I say.

"Nobody wants it to happen."

"It will not happen," I insist. Each of my words punches the air.

"Our leader is driven. It isn't about caring about the feelings of one person—not you, not me, not anyone. It's about protecting the entire planet in a near impossible situation." He sighs. "You need to understand that. You need to understand the stakes."

"Got it."

"You sure?"

I pull my hand away and start walking, totally bluffing. "Of course."

He sighs behind me. The world seems to sigh with him.

"Are you coming?" I call back to China, slowing my pace a tiny bit so as not to be rude. "I know you're just the messenger and it doesn't come from you. You aren't the one I'm mad at."

In fact, his silence now makes sense and in a weird way it makes me feel better that he wasn't the one hesitating.

"I know it's insulting," he says, quickly catching up to me as we enter the elevator. "They have trust issues, that is what it comes down to."

"We all have trust issues," I snark as China and Enoch settle next to me. There's just enough room for all of us.

"It's the state of the world." The doors close.

"Not the state of the universe?" I ask.

"That, too."

Enoch barks once and then sits at my feet.

"That dog is remarkable," China says. "So are you. Big breaths, okay? We'll get through this."

"Of course we will," I say, but inside I'm not quite so sure. The elevator feels almost motionless and I am silent for a moment. We all are. Enoch pants a bit, but that's it. When the doors open again, I think I'm ready for anything—science building with blank white walls and the smell of hot electrical wires overheating in multiple computer hard drives, military compound with steel, reinforced walls and oppressive feeling of death . . . but instead the elevator door opens to a bright, well-lit room. Blue light beams move up and down from the walls, touching us.

"It's security. Just be still," China says.

"Name?" A voice asks from the wall. "All of them."

"Patrick Kinsella. Mana Trent. Dog currently named Enoch. History unknown," China says. It's more of an announcement really.

Enoch grumbles.

I admire her.

"Cleared. Please proceed," the voice says. "They are waiting in the red room."

China places a hand at the small of my back and starts walking forward toward the empty wall.

"China?" I say as he just keeps striding.

"Hologram." He pops through the wall and disappears, then sticks his hand through it and wiggles his fingers. "Come on."

I yank in a breath and step into the wall, ready for my face to hit wood and someone to start laughing like it's all some big practical joke. But I go right through and step into a hallway that's full of dark, rich mahogany wood, high ceilings. A red Afghani carpet lines the floor, stretching on forever in an intricate, ornate design. It's like some sort of billionaire's old house, if the billionaire is old-money billionaire and likes the style of old English manors and Gothic mysteries.

China stands there in the middle of the hall, waiting.

I whistle for Enoch. She hops through the wall, which looks like a door from this side.

China smiles at us. "They've designed the rooms in a way that is homey and sort of Victorian chic. They think it calms people. In retrospect, I think the strangeness sets people on edge, so be prepared."

I could care less about the room's design and décor. "Who are we meeting?" I ask.

"Probably the head of our organization, Julia Bloomsbury, and the lead scientist, Jon Hill."

"The head is a woman?"

"Are you surprised? I thought you were a feminist."

"Surprised in a good way," I say as we stop outside a black-painted door. It shines.

"Be prepared to be surprised again," he says, opening the door.

I almost gasp when I peer inside because the room isn't *just* Victorian chic, it is huge and glamorous, if you're into that sort of thing. The ceilings are easily twenty feet tall. Giant windows with muntins separating them into 144 panes extend up the far wall, revealing the darkness of the outside world. Between the windows are dark-red wallpapered beams that support a paneled ceiling. White carpets are scattered along the dark wood floor. There are wooden desks, ornate Queen Anne chairs, Tiffany lamps, golden-framed portraits. Huge crystal chandeliers dangle from the ceiling.

"Are we in a castle?" I whisper. "We're still in the United States, right?"

He sort of laughs, but not really. It's more a chortle. I don't have any time to respond because two people are approaching us. One is a tall woman with long reddish hair and dark skin. She eyes us and smiles, but it isn't a happy smile. Behind her is a nondescript white man with dark hair and eyes, and a distinct lack of a smile. They are both dressed like white-collar office workers.

"China. This must be Mana," the woman says, extending her hand.

We shake hands and everyone is quickly introduced. As I scan the surroundings, uneasiness makes me a little jittery, which Julia Bloomsbury must notice because she pats a chesterfield couch and indicates that she wants us to sit down. I perch on the edge of a leather cushion, ready to spring, while China just relaxes into the couch like he's suddenly Captain Casual.

Over at a table, Jon Hill, the scientist guy, starts pouring glasses of water. Our fingers touch when he hands it to me and there's something in his eyes that seems . . . It's like he's trying to tell me something telepathically, but I'm not getting it. I don't drink any water, but China does. It seems he's more trusting than I am right now.

"Tell us about your day," Julia says, sitting down and crossing one leg over the other.

China begins. I add to the story. I don't mention the crystal.

Her lips press together as we tell it and she asks the occasional question until I finally can't stand it anymore.

"I'd like to know why you don't think I can be involved," I blurt. "It's pretty obvious that I'm already involved."

"That's not what we think. It's not about involvement. It's about access and trust. We think that you can't be an agent. You're an unknown, Mana. Human but enhanced. We don't know what they did to you—not all of it, at least. Melissa Trent, who you know as your mother, bless her heart, has been watching you all this time, but—"

"My mother was taking care of me, not watching me," I interrupt.

"You have a temper." She arches an eyebrow.

"I have a temper when people distort the truth to suit their agenda. Yes. And I also have a temper when there are hate crimes, bigotry, and people are cruel to animals or my friends."

She chuckles and turns to China. "She's very self-aware."

"In certain ways."

I want to shout *I am right here!* but I'm trying not to show my temper, especially when they are talking about it. Instead I say, "I think I've been alive long enough and been involved enough that I can be trusted."

"No one can be trusted," she snaps.

"Well, I'll fit right in, then." I cross my legs, mimicking her posture. Enoch sniffs at my glass of water. I lower it for her and she laps the liquid out pretty daintily for a dog. I swear the Julia woman looks like she might faint.

"This," Jon says. "This is why she should be here. Look at that."

"The dog?" Julia asks.

"She shows it love." He raises his hands as if that explains everything, but we all give him clueless looks. He groans. "She's obviously kind."

"Kindness doesn't win wars," Julia snaps.

"Kindness wins hearts," he retorts. "'No act of kindness, no matter how small, is ever wasted' or something. Aesop. Or maybe Taylor Swift?"

Julia leaps up into standing position, pacing away. "Two potential agents with kindness in their hearts were brainwashed today. Do not tell me about kindness."

Standing by the windows, she stares out into the darkness. I try to catch China's eye but he keeps looking straight ahead. Something inside my brain clicks and I get it. Jon Hill clears his throat.

"Are you talking about Lyle and Seppie?" I ask. "*They* are potential agents but I'm not? The camp they were going to was agent camp? Is there such a thing as agent camp? Holy—"

China gives a quick nod. "It wasn't my call, but yes."

"You all kept this from me?" I demand. "Even when I specifically asked you? You just lied. You pretended Lyle could be a skin walker, a shapeshifter. You misled me."

Bile rises in my esophagus and hits the back of my throat. My hands clench from anger, or maybe betrayal.

"You are not some special snowflake that gets to know the inner workings and hirings of our agency," Julia snaps at me, not even bothering to turn from the window to deliver the dis. This enflames my anger even more. "He was following my orders."

"Your orders?" I gape at her. I know I'm gaping. I do not care. "What is wrong with you?"

"Do *not* be insolent. This is exactly why we can't trust you. Why you can't be an agent. You have no respect for authority." She turns to face me finally.

"My respect has to be earned."

"And so does mine," she counters, staring at me like she is some sort of alpha dog trying to get me to back down.

"You aren't even giving me a chance to earn it. Why them?" The question sputters out. Anger has overtaken me. Anger and resentment. Who is this woman to decide whether or not I'm worthy? Who is this woman to put my friends in danger without including me?

"They already know about us. The girl is brilliant. The boy is alien, totally infiltrated into society and fast, smart, with no anger issues." She gives a little sigh and breaks her gaze. "Jon, I find this conversation tedious. Why don't you show Miss Trent to her room and explain things while I talk to China here."

Jon perks up, walks forward, and beckons for me to follow him. I feel dismissed, but I don't actually mind. I've already made my mind up about China and my mother's employer. I don't need to waste any more time in some fancy room with people condemning me for nothing while giving me some old-lady version of a mean-girl stare-down.

I follow Jon out into the corridor and Enoch trots by my side, which I appreciate. At least someone is loyal. I'm fuming inside. Lyle and Seppie were both being recruited by China and my mom's employer, the employer that I was supposed to be working with, and neither of them told me. Seppie's whole camp thing was a total lie. And Lyle? Was this part of the reason he was acting so strangely? And why were they at the hospital instead of wherever the camp is? Did they even make it to the camp?

I try to push all the anger and betrayal out of my head as I follow Jon Hill. As we pass old portraits and dark, heavy wood doors, I try not to notice my own insufficiencies, which are kind of glaring in a place like this. My jeans are dirty. My hair is dirty and possibly tangled. I need a shower and clothes. I need a hoity-toity vocabulary. I need to know what's going on.

"Jon," I say, "are you authorized to actually tell me what's happening, or are you just sort of my chaperone to my room? I do have a room, right? Or is she kicking me out?"

"You have a room," he says demurely, but then his brown eyes twinkle. "For the night at least . . ."

"You're a tease, aren't you?"

"I used to be. Then I started working here . . ." He opens a door to a room that I would classify as lavish-hotel style. The bed is large with an upholstered headboard and the room as high-end fancy as the room we were just talking in. Four throw pillows lean against four posh sleeping pillows, and the bed is tastefully covered in a sort of beige-gold comforter and duvet set. There's a Queen Anne settee against a wall. A door appears to lead to the bathroom. Jeans and an Irish fisherman's sweater, thick wool socks, a tan vest that seems fleece lined, and a dark green jersey shirt are laid out on the bed.

"Clothes?" I ask.

"We thought you might be in need of a change of wardrobe," Jon says, striding across the room and pulling shut the drapes. I grab a pen off the dresser and scrawl across my hand, *Are they listening?*

When he turns, he sees what I've written and mouths the word yes.

I scrawl out, *Cameras?*

He mouths the word no, and then says, in a slightly too loud voice, "If you care to shower, which I imagine you do, the bathroom is through the doors to your left. The closet is to your right." He takes my pen and writes on my hand, *Wash this off. Trust nobody.*

Not even you? I write back, but aloud I say, "Do I smell?"

It is the only thing I can think to say to cover the silence.

Jon snorts and says, "I would never tell a lady such a thing." He blathers on, "So, if you need anything tonight, I would suggest you pick up the phone by the head of your bed and just ask. Either I or a young man named Steven Boucher will answer your requests. I am on duty until midnight and then it is Steven's turn. Breakfast will be served promptly at seven in the morning. If you miss it, there are no warming stations. The dining area is down the hall to the left and to the right and to the left, third door." When he's speaking, he writes something on my other hand.

"That's complicated." I give him big eyes.

"Everything is complicated or convoluted here," he says.

"Can you tell me why I'm not considered worthy enough to be an agent? Am I a captive here?" I blurt.

"Of course not. And it isn't my place. I will say that our agents are picked with absolute discretion. And I am not the one who makes those choices, sadly." He winks, hands me back my pen, and folds my fingers into my palm. "Again, please let me know if you need anything, but I am only on duty until midnight, then must sleep before I have more sciencing to do. Have a lovely shower."

He bounds out the door and shuts it quietly behind him. I stare at it. It locks. I am obviously a captive. Grumbling and confused, I slowly uncurl my fingers so I can read what he's written on my hand. The printing is small but legible. I wonder if he does this often.

I gasp when I read it.

You need to leave.

   She plans on killing you.

   Go before midnight. I left the window unlocked. Change into these clothes. I have stripped them of tracking devices. There is a clean car by the main road, left of entrance, hidden in bush.

   China does not know. They feel he is too attached to be trusted.

   Use the crystal.

   Find the others.

   Do not become what they fear you might be.

"Holy . . ." I whisper.

Enoch whines.

Jon knows about the crystal. Does Julia, too?

"I don't want to leave China," I whisper.

Enoch whines again.

"Do you think I have time for a shower?"

Enoch walks to the window and hits it with her paw.

"Fine," I say and begin changing my clothes. "Fine. It just would be nice to feel clean for once." I rethink this as I pull off my shirt. "Clean and not hunted. And safe. It would be nice to feel safe."

Enoch doesn't say anything, just sits and waits and tilts her doggy head like this is the sort of self-involved whining that she doesn't have time for. I get it. I don't have time for it either.

CHAPTER 10

The decision to trust a total stranger or not to trust them is kind of a gut reaction, an instinct, and I don't waste time second-guessing myself as I run through the woods outside of the mansion-slash-compound-slash-whatever. Jon Hill wrote on my hand to use the crystal and to leave. He said that they want to kill me—not China, but the organization. The question is *why*. Why would they want to kill me? It has to do with their worrying about what I might become, I guess.

Okay.

And he wants me to use the crystal to find the others. As I narrowly avoid slamming into a tree trunk, I think about when I activated the crystal. There was a guy. I saw a guy who could potentially be dead. He must be one of the people I need to find. But why?

No idea.

And there was the other guy—I only saw the back of his head—who was in that medical room that was all creepy.

How did Jon Hill even know about the crystal? Nobody is supposed to know about the crystal.

Jon Hill is probably risking a lot letting me escape.

Enoch the dog seemed to agree with his assessment of things, so I am still not second-guessing my decision. I just feel a bit bad leaving China.

China doesn't know. The words are still on my hand. Why wouldn't they tell one of their best employees their plans? Who are these people?

"They suck," I whisper to Enoch.

Enoch sits abruptly. I stop. "What? Is it a Wendigo?"

Enoch flattens on her belly. She hits me with her paw.

"You want me to hide?"

Just then a motor rumbles, a softness getting louder and closer. I slam down to the ground next to the dog. She gives me five. Lights slash through the trees and the ground vibrates beneath me.

"Bad guys?" I whisper.

She doesn't answer.

"You want me to be quiet?"

She still doesn't answer, which I take as an affirmative in the dog world of interspecies communication. I sigh. My junior year of high school should be full of cheering competitions, bad dances, studying, and stressing about college. Instead, I am flat on the cold, snow-frosted forest floor talking to a dog, possibly running for my life. Strike that. I am almost definitely running for my life. I'm trusting the advice of a random stranger, running from the people I wanted to work for and help. And what am I running to? That's the next big question.

When we can no longer hear the car's engine, Enoch stands back up. I follow her lead and rush along parallel to the road, a few feet into the woods, but not so far that I will get lost. We break out on the main road.

"He wrote that the car is to the left of the entrance," I announce, but Enoch has already turned her doggy self and she heads straight for some brush. "Here?"

She barks, which I take as a good sign because she finally feels safe enough to make noise.

All around us is darkness and quiet. The cold bites into my skin. A quick check of my phone tells me it is eleven, but it feels later.

I start pulling the pine boughs off a dark-colored car that looks like it's some sort of electric hybrid, newer model. Sap sticks to my hands and probably ruins what Jon Hill wrote on my skin. I think I have the words memorized now, though.

You need to leave.

She plans on killing you.

Why would they want to kill me? Why am I such a threat? They have agents like China, and future agents like Seppie and Lyle. Bile fills my throat. It's hard not to be chosen. It's hard always to be the one who is the worst. Lyle is the best at running and making friends. Seppie is the best at school and life. I am only the best at flying and tumbling, and that's just because aliens enhanced me. This is what I'm obsessing about as Enoch drags some limbs off, using her mouth and walking backward.

"You are an amazing dog," I whisper.

Her tail wags. I push away my feelings of inadequacy as best as I can and try to focus on what is happening right now. The words on my hand. Escape.

Go before midnight.

It's super-obvious that I have to hurry. It's getting close to midnight, I know. What if Jon's relief has to drive in? Someone will see me. I start pulling the boughs off at a faster rate.

China does not know.

Use the crystal.

Find the others.

Do not become what they fear you might be.

What the hell does that honestly mean? The crystal is in a pocket on my vest, zipped up and safe. I hadn't even told China about it, but somehow Jon Hill knows. I finally get enough boughs off the car to open the driver's side door.

"Hop in!" I order Enoch.

She doesn't.

I feel bad for being bossy. She's such an exceptional dog, so I soften my voice and say, "Sweetie, we have to go."

She whines, pawing at the snow by the car's back tires. Suddenly, the world seems still and cold and full of danger all over again. There's got to be a reason she won't just jump in the car.

"What is it?" I whisper as I take my phone and turn on the flashlight app, checking out the front of the car. It seems fine, but how would I know what to expect? Then I let the light sweep the back and my breath comes out in a horrible rush.

There's a body in the backseat, facing the back of the car so I can't see his face, but I recognize the jeans and the jacket and the short, shaggy hair and my heart flutters.

"Lyle!"

I'm in the car without a second thought, trying to free him, pulling at the duct tape around his ankles, which is pretty freaking impossible to tear. I find the end and start unwrapping it.

"Enoch, help me," I demand even though Enoch is a dog and I don't know how I expect her to help. But she actually does. She rips at the duct tape with her super-sharp dog teeth and makes easy work of it. I flip Lyle around, abandoning the duct tape encircling his hands to Enoch's superior abilities. She tears right through it again as I rip off the tape over his lips. I remove some of the skin with it and I'd apologize if Lyle wasn't already swearing and shouting.

"We have to go. Mana, we've got to go," he insists, scrambling into a sitting position. "What's with the dog?"

"The dog is mine." I move into the driver's seat as Lyle scoots past Enoch into the passenger seat. He rubs at his shoulders as I close the doors. "Thanks. Start the car. Let's go."

This is the same person who just a few hours ago tried to attack me with a crowbar, and a few hours before that broke up with me. So, no, I don't go. "Dude, you have to tell me what's going on."

"Seppie," he sighs out. "This guy took Seppie. He left me here as a present, he said. . . ." Lyle unleashes a volley of swear words that would get him grounded for life if his mom wasn't in a containment cell somewhere.

"What guy?" My palms tingle and my vision blurs. Not again. Not Seppie.

"Large, angry, but calm all at once. He said that China's people want to kill you but that you'd escape. He said that he was leaving me here as a good-faith present. He said that you'd understand that the time of humans is almost over. He sucked." He pauses. "Can you start the car?"

"There's no key."

"You push a button." He points at a button.

"Oh." I pause and do not push the button. "Do you remember trying to kill me?"

"Sorry about that."

"Do you know *why* you tried to kill me?"

"I think I was trying to kidnap you, not kill you."

Relief floods me, but I'm still not 100 percent about this situation, not with everything that's already happened. I have to be cautious, no matter how psyched I am to have rescued Lyle and to actually be interacting with him in a normalish way—well, normal for us. So I ask, "Is that what you're doing now? Trying to kidnap me?"

"What? No . . . Not at all. I . . ." He pauses and lets his head fall back against the headrest. "This is all so confusing, but I don't think so."

I press the button, starting the car. "Tell me what you know and apologize."

"I'm sorry I tried to kidnap you."

"No, you couldn't help that. Apologize for being an ass at school. Why did you do that? That hurt."

"Oh," he says. "That . . ."

"Yeah, that."

I pull out onto the road and just start driving. I don't know where we're going other than away, and for right this second that is good enough.

"That," he says, rubbing at his forearms, "is all part of the story."

"Well, start telling it, then," I say.

And he does.

CHAPTER 11

It was a woman who approached Lyle just a couple of weeks ago. He'd been running down by the country club. She stepped out from behind the side of the main building and fell in front of him. She'd watched him long enough to know that he was the sort of guy who would stop if someone seemed hurt.

"They'd been watching you?" I ask as I drive down the dark road.

"All of us."

I stare ahead of me, too nervous for some reason to really look at Lyle. "And that didn't creep you out?"

"It did and it didn't. I sort of figured that someone had us under observation since you are what you are and I am what I am, you know?"

"I know." But I hadn't been the one thinking about it. Maybe China's boss was right. Maybe I'm not agent material. Depression settles in my stomach. Bile rises in my throat. I bet agents have stronger stomachs than I do. I bet agents think about people watching them. I push all the anxiety and doubt away and try to focus on driving and Lyle and Seppie.

"So, what happened?"

"She said she was recruiting for China's agency, the one your mom worked for," he tells me. "She said you were in danger."

"Ha. Danger from them," I sputter.

"Disdainful much?"

"Disdainful a lot," I answer and give him a quick rundown of what's happened before he continues with his story.

"And you trust this Jon Hill?" he asks.

"Enoch trusts him, I think. But I'm not a hundred percent sure."

"Enoch is a dog."

Enoch makes a noise.

"Enoch is special," I retort. "But she does like China."

"Maybe China is villainous."

"That makes no sense. China isn't a bad guy! Enoch wouldn't like him if he was. And you don't really think so either. You let yourself be recruited for the agency."

"I know, but let's face it, Mana. We don't know who's a good guy and who's a bad guy. Maybe we're the bad guys." He cracks his neck, which he's been complaining is stiff from being tied up in the back of the car. "It's all perspective. I mean, when a shark eats a surfer, the shark's friends are cheering him on because he's got food to survive."

"In someone else's story, we probably *are* the bad guys," I admit. "The two annoying cheerleaders who refuse to do what they are supposed to, to trust who they are supposed to trust. They could cause the end of the world if they aren't careful."

He doesn't say anything.

"What? Is that wrong?"

"I was too busy gulping to respond." He sighs. "I don't want that to be what we are."

"What do you want us to be?" I ask and honestly, I'm asking because it's a perfect time for him to say *a couple.*

"Best friends, like Captain America and Bucky or Achilles and Patroklos, only with Seppie, too, of course. Three friends meant to save the world and each other." He must feel my mood shift because he goes, "What?"

"Those are guys." I don't add, *and they aren't romantic.* Although,

I think something may have been going on with Cap and Bucky and also with Achilles and Patroklos.

"Oh." He is silent. "Are there dynamic women world-saving duos or trios?"

"You're the geeky one. You should know."

"Xena and Gabriel?"

"I have no idea who they are," I admit. "I need some girl-power schooling. Like, if the world survives."

"We all do."

"Back to your story," I insist, trying to ignore all my sad feelings about romance and Lyle's lack of it. "Who put you here? Tell me about the guy."

"He was bulky, strong. Military, I think, not super-old, not a lot of hair. He could have been a cop, I guess. It was his attitude. He took us after—after we tried to capture you at the hospital."

"I'm already trying to forget that." You don't want to remember your friends coming at you with crowbars.

He rubs his eyes, and his voice is hoarse. He grabs my hand with his free hand and holds it, wrapping his fingers around my fingers. It feels . . . good and right. He says, "Me, too."

After a second, I ask, "What was it like?"

"I could feel him in my brain, you know? I could feel him trying to control me."

So, the mind controller wasn't Pierce. It was a man.

"Trying?"

"Okay. Controlling me." His fingers tighten around mine and then let go of my hand altogether. His voice shakes a bit with anger, or maybe embarrassment. In the dark of the car, it's hard to tell. Plus, I'm focused on the winding road. But the distress in Lyle's voice breaks my heart as he continues, "And I tried to fight him and I couldn't and then it all just went hazy while we were trying to get you. I tried to fight him and my head felt like it was exploding. Like I literally thought it was exploding. We chased after you again and

I fought him again and I wake up and I'm in the back of a truck—some sort of box truck—and Seppie's there, too. We're both bound up. He and some other guy open the back doors and he's smiling, happy. He points at me and says, 'You are the present,' and he points at Seppie and says, 'You are the toy. Or maybe I should say *bait*.'"

"Toy." My stomach turns, but I'm actually a tiny bit relieved. All of this means that the mind controller was male. That means it definitely wasn't Pierce. "Why were you guys at the hospital?"

"We got a message that you needed us. So we left camp—Seppie had only just got there, too . . ." He pauses. "The counselors were not happy."

"You guys got in trouble for me?"

"Yeah . . ." He is quiet for a second. "We need to find her. He left me in that car hours ago. They could be anywhere."

"And where do we look?"

"Food?" Lyle suggests. "Let's stop for food and figure it out."

"I don't really want to waste time, Lyle."

"It's midnight and we have no idea where to even begin."

"Fine. What's open?"

"Denny's or something. There's got to be a Denny's. Or we could go to a convenience store somewhere."

"Do you even know where we are?" I ask.

"Maine? Canada? Vermont?" He peers into the darkness. "Somewhere with a lot of trees."

"It can't be Vermont. We haven't been driving that long. I think we were just up north by the border of Maine and New Hampshire." I decide that our first goal should be to figure out where we are. Our next goal should be to find some food. Our third goal is to figure out what to do on the bigger scale of things, which means rescuing Seppie and hearing the rest of Lyle's story.

The first goal is simple because it turns out there's a GPS in the car.

"Can't they track us if we turn it on?" I ask.

"Possibly. But we could just turn it on for a second."

We do. It appears that we are actually still in New Hampshire, just northern New Hampshire, in the White Mountains. My mom's ancestors were the white people who settled here. There were other people who lived in these mountains for twelve thousand years before white Europeans came, but nobody ever mentions them. But they were the Abenaki, linguistically Algonquian, and pretty cool people, which I tell Lyle once we realize that we're by Willey Mountain and if we follow the highway, we can probably get to food in less than a half hour.

"You always say you're stupid, Mana, but you know a lot about things. That's history right there."

"Not the kind we get tested on."

"True."

"I'll find the convenience store. You finish telling me what's been happening to you," I suggest as I switch the GPS back off and continue through Crawford Notch on Route 302. If it wasn't so dark, we would be able to stare up at the snow-covered mountains and down at Saco River, which sort of follows the two-lane highway. Mom loved it up here. Even without the GPS, I know that we're headed for Attitash Mountain Resort and the town of Bartlett. There has to be a convenience store there.

"So, the woman tells me all about the organization and how they have successfully incorporated aliens, such as Pierce, who we met if you remember—"

"Of course I remember. Don't be insulting."

He talks right over me. "—and how they think that I am sympathetic to humanity's cause and should be incorporated into the organization as well."

"So they recruited you."

"Basically."

"And you didn't tell me because?"

I swear he actually stutters. "Because . . . because . . . they told me not to? And I wanted to figure out what was going on? I knew I could convince them to take you in too eventually, because you're awesome, obviously, and China had told you that you would be able to help, but then they said . . ."

"They said what?"

"That you were unstable and too risky. They said they had determined more information about your usefulness and it looked like you were too much of a risk."

"Because . . ."

"They didn't tell me the *because*. I asked, though. I asked a lot." He touches my shoulder. "Don't be mad."

"Of course I'm mad! You didn't even trust me enough to tell me what was going on. That's a big deal, Lyle."

He says nothing.

"I thought we were friends. Cap and Bucky."

He still says nothing.

"Xena and Gabriel. Kirk and Spock," I rattle on, totally annoyed. "Say something."

"There's nothing to say. You're right. I was an ass. I thought I was protecting you and—"

"I don't need protecting!" I shout. Enoch barks, in support, I think. "I'm not the one who got brainwashed. I'm not the one who was tied up in the back of a car. I'm not the one who abandons her friends because she got a damn job offer."

"You swore."

"I'm mad."

"You never swear."

"I'm never this mad." My hands tighten around the steering wheel.

This is truth. Anger courses through my muscles. Every neuron in my body feels . . . it's hard to describe, but the closest word is *electrified*. I feel electrified. How could they possibly act like I'm the one who needs protecting when I am the only one who doesn't get kidnapped or knocked unconscious or . . .

"Agh!" The word explodes out of me. "You told me that you couldn't do us anymore? What is that supposed to mean?"

I slam my fist into the dashboard. The dashboard cracks.

"Mana." Lyle's voice is quiet but obviously trembling. "Um . . . maybe you should pull over."

"Just tell me what you meant when you said you couldn't do us anymore."

"I don't know. I already told you I don't know, didn't I? I just . . . I couldn't lie about the camp and be a couple. You can't be with someone you're lying to. It made me feel all gross inside."

"Not good enough, Lyle." The words come out through gritted teeth and I yank the car to the side of the mountain road. There's a lot of snow up here and barely a breakdown lane so even though I am trying to be stealthy, I throw on the hazard lights. There is no point in having us and a car destroyed by another driver who doesn't see us in the dark night.

"Mana, you're kind of worrying me."

"Why? Do you think I'll kidnap you? Betray you for a job opportunity? Lie to you? Because I'm not going to, Lyle. Do you know why? Because I know how to be a friend and a girlfriend, unlike you, who have dated pretty much every girl in school except me and Seppie."

I throw open the door and hop out into the night. The light from the car's interior illuminates things. I slip on some tiny patch of black ice and scream in frustration, but instead of falling, I do some sort of side aerial. The motion shakes the crystal out of my pocket and right into my hand. My fingers wrap around it instinctively. Anger just rips through me. We are up against so much—aliens, agencies that betray us, some random guy who has kidnapped my best friend as bait. Bait. Like she isn't human. Like she's a toy, something to be used. And if she had trusted me—if they both had trusted me—maybe this wouldn't have been the result. Who knows? I'm not just fighting against aliens, I'm fighting against my whole entire life.

Lyle opens his door as I land. He peers out. His voice is quiet. "Are you okay?"

"Of course I'm okay. I'm a genetically enhanced freak whose mom is in a coma, whose pretend dad is missing, and whose friends betrayed her, whose boyfriend dumped her because he felt gross inside, and now one of those friends is kidnapped. I am one hundred percent okay."

"So . . . you're not okay." Lyle steps gingerly around the front of the car toward me, without falling. "I'm sorry."

"For what?" I glare at him, huffing like I'm some sort of Big Bad Wolf, some sort of monster. But I'm just me, Mana, cheerleading freak, toyed with by aliens, lied to for forever. It hurts too much to keep thinking about.

"For not being honest with you?" he offers, hands spread wide open.

"It sounds better when you don't make your apology into a question."

His hands drop and he actually scowls at me. "You know what sounds better? When you don't pick apart someone's apology and make it not an apology."

"It wasn't a real apology."

"How do you know? You aren't in my head."

"It. Was. A. Question!" I holler and all my anger come thundering out of me like some sort of sine wave or something. It is physical and green and you can see it.

You can *see* it.

"Lyle! Duck!"

He dives out of the way as the wave of my anger hits the car. The car disintegrates when the wave hits it. The wave rumbles into darkness. And the anger inside of me is gone—just gone—replaced by terror.

"Enoch! Where is Enoch?" I scream into the newer, deeper darkness. This has never happened before. Why is this happening?

The crystal in my hand shimmies and falls into the snow a few feet in front of me. Enoch rushes out from behind where the car was, whining, tail between her legs. I squat down. "Here, baby . . . Come here, baby."

"I'm totally all right. Thanks for caring," Lyle says, standing up and brushing snow off his pants.

Enoch licks my face. I let her. Having her there calms me. I wrap my arms around her and breathe in her doggy smell.

"Sorry . . ." I start to apologize to Lyle. "I'm not sure what—"

"Yeah. Maybe that's why they don't trust you."

I bristle. "Nice."

"You know it's true."

I do, but whatever. Having some sort of adrenaline-based power that I know nothing about doesn't mean I should be put to death, which I start to explain to Lyle, but he's too busy whining about me vaporizing the car and how now we're going to have to walk and how cold it is and why this has never happened before and so on.

"You're a runner," I say. "You can run a marathon. You can walk two miles to a town."

"But it's dark and cold. And we need to find Seppie."

"First we need to find the crystal," I say, "but you're right. We do need to find Seppie."

Something moves in the darkness.

"What's that?"

Enoch barks.

"The crystal?" Lyle's suggestion is a question, just like his apology.

I bite my tongue. There's no use fighting with Lyle about his betrayal right now. We're in this together, or at least we should be, and honestly, I need all the help I can get. If I vaporized a car because I was angry, my emotions are a little out of control. Plus, you always do better rescuing people if you have friends with you to help.

Lyle's by my side now, squatting down next to me. Enoch licks his face, but he doesn't really see. Instead, he points to the general area where the crystal fell into the snow. "I know we have to get Seppie, figure out where she is, but something . . . whatever that crystal thing is, something is going on with it."

He's right. The crystal makes a whirring noise.

"You hear that?" I ask, peering into the darkness.

"Yep . . . It sounds like . . . It sounds like . . . There!" Lyle points in front of us and slightly to the right and there it is. The crystal. It hovers above the snow. It isn't as high as it was when I was at school and it shot up to the ceiling. It's only levitating about three feet into the air.

"Should I get it?" I ask.

"I don't know."

"Enoch?"

Lyle squints at me. "You're asking the dog?"

"I'm not one hundred percent sure she's a regular dog," I admit. "She seems to communicate a lot."

Before I can explain the rest of my observations about Enoch, the crystal spins, emitting a light.

Lyle gasps. "It's a hologram."

"But what is it showing us?" I ask as the images begin to take shape.

There's the back of a man's head again—square, crew cut. Beyond him there's a girl, strapped to a table. Fully clothed, thank god, but in some sort of hospital garb. Almost like what nurses wear—made of that weird material and with drawstring pants.

"Is that Seppie?" Lyle asks, stepping forward. "I'm pretty sure that's the guy who put me in the car. Yeah . . . yeah . . . that's the back of his head."

Enoch growls and Lyle stops babbling.

"Usually they can hear me. Maybe we're too far away." I step into the deep snow toward the crystal just as the man jerks forward toward Seppie. The back of his head is the same as the man's when I used the crystal before and saw that hospital room. What is he doing to Seppie? Horror takes my voice, but I find it again in a whisper, "Where are they?"

And then the crystal moves again, spinning. It's an outside shot of what looks like a YMCA on the outskirts of a town. Behind it is a brick building, a crosswalk and sidewalk in front of it, marked with evenly spaced trees, branches naked from winter.

"Whoa," Lyle whispers. "It's like your personal Google Earth or something."

"I guess. It's never done this before. I've seen people but not places."

"Do you know how to work it? We need to know where this is."

"No idea," I say, but I move closer to the hologram, trying to figure it out. Enoch stays close at my heels.

The YMCA is aluminum-sided, gray and squat, and not too big, with a flat roof and a green racing stripe near the top of it. The picture whirls around and I can see the sign with the Y logo blasted across a silhouette of an island. Underneath, there are letters spelling out MOUNT DESERT ISLAND.

"Is that where she is?" I gasp.

"It must be. Why else would it be showing us?"

"I don't understand how the crystal is showing us things at all," I say as it flies back toward me. I grab it and stare. It looks normal, just warm and nice in my hands.

"It's like it can divine your thoughts or something," Lyle suggests as I pet the crystal with two fingers.

"Good crystal. Good crystal," I croon.

"It's not a dog, Mana," Lyle scolds.

Enoch grumbles.

"If it's sentient, I want to be nice to it," I explain as I tuck it back into my pocket and plow out of the snow and back onto the road. "I mean, it's trying to help us, I think. That's super-nice."

"That looked like a military compound, not a YMCA," Lyle says.

"So we need troops," I add, walking down the road. "We need to infiltrate that place, get Seppie back, and get on with things. But I think it was just a Y. They are in there somewhere, some back room or something."

He ignores most of what I've said and asks, "What sorts of things do we have to get on with?"

"Saving-the-world-and-humanity sorts of things," I say, "but it looks like we're going to have to depend on ourselves. Not Mom and China's agency. Not the government's Men in Black. Just us. Are you with me, Lyle?"

"I thought you didn't trust me." His voice is rough and low with emotion.

He's by my side, walking with me, and he's right. I didn't trust him because I knew something was off, but I can't let a week or so of weirdness ruin a lifetime of friendship. It's not as if I feel all rah-rah-Lyle at the moment, but he's still my friend and I need him. I need him to rescue Seppie. But I also really want him to kiss me again, right now and here, to have him just do it. But he isn't even facing me. He's staring straight ahead and it's obvious that some declaration of love isn't going to happen. I have to be mature about that, right? It's better to save a friendship with Lyle than to have nothing.

"You betrayed me," I say, "but I get why. I just wish you had told me what was going on. It hurt, Lyle."

"I know. I'm sorry. I . . . It was the wrong choice."

His apology is way better now. We both know it. I tuck my hand into his arm as we fast walk down the mountain road. "Forgiven."

CHAPTER 12

We walk down the icy, dark road as quickly as we can. No other cars come. No headlights slice through the darkness. No tires crunch across the salty, gravel roadway. We use my cell as a flashlight. The signal doesn't work, but the light still does. Enoch trots calmly beside us, not even on a leash. I worry about the road salt and sand hurting her paws, but she seems fine. As we travel, Lyle gives me a few more details about what he knows and what he's done.

"There's a whole training center," he tells me. "They have Futures."

"Futures?"

"Future agents. I wanted to call us Futures, but that was done in *Buffy*, I guess. I wanted it to be an homage. Anyways, I was the only alien. I went there last weekend."

A sickening feeling fills my heart when I think about how he got to go and how he'd said he was at Dartmouth for some sort of sub-frosh, early acceptance weekend.

"They should have let you go, too," he says.

I'm not sure what to say to that. So I just say, "You've already said that."

"I know. I just—"

"Feel like a dick?" I suggest.

"Pretty much," he admits.

I decide to let it go. "So, where was this place?"

"Portsmouth."

Portsmouth is an artsy little city right on the Maine and New Hampshire border. It's full of brick buildings and theater people who spell *theater* with an *re* at the end. It's a good place to spend New Year's Eve because there are free events everywhere, including ice sculpture contests and fireworks. Seppie always loved the ice sculptures. Just thinking about her fills me with worry.

Lyle keeps talking. The camp happens on the weekends until full integration is achieved and then it's a weeklong thing. Most of the campers initially think the training is premilitary and don't really know it's about aliens. The camp directors tell them after the initiation, a couple weeks into the program.

"Seppie and I were the exceptions," he admits.

"They mentioned you guys being recruited at the compound. I didn't really want to believe it. And Seppie admitted today that she was going away. She said it was for something else, though. She lied."

"We weren't supposed to tell anyone."

"I'm not *anyone*." Then I ask the question I don't really want answered even though I've already asked China himself. "And China was okay with it?"

Lyle gives me the answer I really don't want. "Yeah, I guess."

No wonder Seppie told me to stop texting him. She knew it was pointless, that I was making a fool out of myself. Shame mixes with anger and it makes me ill inside, like I've eaten too many pizza slices or something.

"He trusted you," Lyle says. "He thought you'd be a great agent, better than me, but he didn't have enough pull. The woman in charge was set against it, he said."

"The woman in charge needs to not be in charge," I say as we finally spot the lights of a town and a gas station. "Bartlett. My mom's mom was a Bartlett."

"My mom's mom was an alien," Lyle says.

And I want to say, "At least you know who your biological

mom is," but that's unfair because it's not his fault I was adopted. Plus, his mom sucks. She was the last person to kidnap Seppie. It's a trend, which I mention as we enter the Circle K gas station-slash-convenience store.

"They know she matters to you. It makes her vulnerable. Makes you vulnerable."

"So, I'm supposed to not have friends?" I blink against the hard glare of the store's overhead lights, which make Lyle's skin sallow.

"Do you think China has friends?"

"My mom?" I suggest, checking on Enoch, who is supposed to be standing guard by the door but is actually licking unmentionable doggy places.

"She didn't really have a ton of friends, not close friends, if you think about it." He sounds apologetic. "And she's in a coma, which is additional proof of how dangerous this all is."

"Good point." I sigh. "First things first. We need to get to Seppie quickly. We have no car."

"And food." Lyle grabs two boxes of Turkey & Cheddar Lunchables, which also feature Capri Sun Pacific Coolers and Skittles.

"Seriously?"

"It's made with 'whole grain.'" He points at the box and moves on to a tube of cookie dough.

"That's raw. We have no oven."

"Right now, I wouldn't think salmonella is about to be the thing that takes us down, and if I'm going out in a blaze of glory, I'm going to go out with a happy stomach."

"A salmonella stomach is not a happy stomach," I say and grab a tin of Nutella. "Look, it's the snack of the gods!"

He picks up a box of Little Debbie's Cosmic Brownies and a bag of Bar-B-Q Fritos. "*This* is a snack of the gods. We have candy-coated chocolate on top of moist brownies coupled with the barbecue awesome crunch of the Fritos."

Staring at the bag and the trippy Little Debbie's box, I sigh. "Do you have any money?"

He makes a face. "Of course."

"Your kidnappers didn't take your money? Or your wallet? Or anything?"

"No." He brings the items up to the counter. The woman there is stone-faced and yawning. "That's probably weird, isn't it?"

"Probably?" I sigh and watch him pay the cashier, and I decide not to comment further until we are back out in the cold with our bag of healthy yumminess. I am kidding here about the healthy part. Then I have a last-minute thought and say, "Hold on!"

Rushing to the back wall, I grab two Pepsi bottles—caffeine—and place them on the counter. "Just in case."

He doesn't disagree. The clerk lady just runs the bar codes over her scanner and makes no comment at all except to announce the total we owe her.

Once we're out I say, "You were actually kidnapped, right? That isn't some lie and elaborate setup?"

"Of course!" He has ripped open the Fritos and is munching through them like a machine.

"You don't know how to get out of duct tape restraints?" I lean against the side of the building and pry open the Cosmic Brownies. I try not to think about all the chemicals in them but I can't avoid it, so I change over to the Lunchable. It probably isn't much better, but at least it has protein.

As if he's reading my thoughts, Lyle says, "You can have my turkey."

"Thank you, Mr. Vegetarian."

"No problem."

Lyle doesn't like to eat things with a face.

"So, at the training place, they didn't teach you about breaking out of duct tape restraints. Did they teach you about what kind of alien you are?"

"They did."

He keeps eating and it isn't until he's done chewing that he says, "I feel a little awkward talking about it, honestly."

My heart plummets. I can't believe he won't tell me. "If you can't tell me, who can you tell, really? Other than Seppie?"

"That's not it. I'm just not into talking about myself."

I scoff. He punches my arm. I punch his and almost drop the contents of the Lunchable, which would be horrific.

"Since when?"

"Since all this started happening? Since I realized I didn't know who I was."

His voice is so sad and so honest. There's no trace of teasing, sarcastic Lyle, no trace of dorky, science fiction–loving Lyle. I offer him a cracker with cheese. He takes it, engulfing it. I've been so focused on my identity crisis, and my mom, and worrying about the eradication of humanity, that I've forgotten about my own humanity, my friends, and how all of this was impacting them.

"You're still the same you, Lyle. Your actions and thoughts are what make you you. It's not about your DNA or your species or whatever."

"Are you trying to give me a pep talk?"

I shrug.

He bumps me with his hip, like old times. "It's better than Mrs. Bray's motivational moments. Do you remember, 'It's about how high we jump and loudly we cheer, so remember we may not dominate the court but we rock the world!'"

Mrs. Bray is our cheer coach. She is the worst pep talker ever. You always feel more depressed afterward.

"Or, 'When you raise your voices, you raise everyone's spirits?'" I groan. "And 'Players get breaks between halves. Cheerleaders are always on! So, be on!'"

"I'm sort of amazed she still coaches. She's nice, though." After a second he says, "How about I tell you more about it when we get to the training camp?"

"Okay. And how are we going to get there?"

Looking up at the dark sky, he smiles. "Well, nobody is going to see us, so I say we fly."

*F*lying isn't really exactly flying. My skill set is more like bounding, *really* bounding. I jump and move about the length of a football field, reaching up high toward the sky, over treetops, before landing and instantly taking off again. I make the space, the sky, the ground, my own, using the darkness to hide who I am, my powers, to get us there more quickly. I imagine my flying-jumping movement is sort of dorky and awkward-looking, but Seppie insisted it was actually cool and graceful. Lyle has to climb on my back so that I can keep him with me.

"No fireman carry?" he asks, referencing the carry where you sling someone over your shoulder and their butt is up toward the sky.

"If you want. . . ." I tease. "Or I can hold you in my arms like grooms carry brides when they cross a threshold."

"Tempting . . ."

But we decide on the piggyback position, which allows Lyle not to get motion sick and also to see where he's going. It's awkward because he's way taller than I am and his legs are sort of dangling.

"Are you strong enough to carry me?" he asks.

"I'm strong enough to carry anyone," I say, because I am. I could even carry China. But I can't carry Enoch *and* Lyle.

Crouching down, I explain the situation to her. She barks at me.

"I think she actually understands you," Lyle says.

"That's not the problem. The problem is that I don't understand her."

"You never learned to speak dog." He shakes his head like this is a terribly disappointing failure on my part.

Smiling up at him, I say, "I've never learned a lot of things."

For a second, I'm a tiny bit jealous of Lyle. He knows where he's from now. He knows what he is. He might not be 100 percent cool with it, but at least he knows. At least they trusted him enough to try to teach him and use him.

Enoch makes a whimpering noise. She hits me with her paw.

"I'm trying." I sigh.

"We have to get going." Lyle fidgets, shifting his weight on his feet. "We need to go to camp, get the others, go to Maine to that YMCA place and save Seppie."

"I'm not leaving Enoch," I insist. "Even if it is to gather the troops."

He lifts his hands up in surrender. "I'm not saying you shou—"

Enoch leaps into his arms and then scurries up and around his neck, dangling there like some sort of giant, furry scarf with jowls and paws. Lyle staggers for a second but keeps his balance and starts laughing. "I think she wants to try this."

So, that's what we do. Enoch stays draped across Lyle's neck and shoulders while he climbs onto my back. I make an appropriate *oomph* noise under their weight but readjust. I take a sip from the Pepsi bottle, just a small one, before recapping it and stashing it in one of the oversize pockets of my vest.

"You guys ready?" I check, and then I take off. "Let's go to that camp and get a bunch of Futures and rescue Seppie."

"Rah. Rah," Lyle monotones.

"No sarcastic cheering allowed," I say, liking the way he has to hug my back. "We can do this."

"Your motivational speech-making just needs a bit of work," he says. I think he's actually sniffing my hair.

"Doesn't everyone's?"

He and Enoch are heavy, but it's doable. My leaps aren't as high as when I first did this with Seppie, but between now and then I've been practicing surreptitiously and I have the movement down pat.

It's almost second nature. Lyle makes a whooping noise, which cracks me up. Seppie thought this was cool, too.

Seppie.

As we move through the trees, I think about her. Before all this happened, Seppie and I were just two random cheerleaders who looked out for each other. In a school full of mostly white kids, we were each other's support system, family. That's how it always was with Lyle, too. We have been friends forever. When everyone else believed I was stupid, Lyle and Seppie didn't. When strangers look at Seppie and think she is some sort of "mad black woman" stereotype, I have her back. When people taunt Lyle for being a cheerleader because it is something "girls do," we verbally kick their ass.

We've always been a team.

And I'm mad at them for messing that up, but I get it. They were protecting me, the same way that I would want to protect them. I understand their motivation even if I don't like their actions. Something hitches inside my throat. I'm so tired of people using my friends as pawns. I'm so tired of this life-or-death crap, this constant confusion about who is bad and who is good, and I blurt all this out to Lyle and Enoch as I bound toward the training camp, following along the highway.

"You feel like you need to choose a side and you don't know which side is good or not?" he yells back, his words battling the wind.

"Exactly." I bounce up again. It is so fast, moving like this; so free.

"So just choose a side."

"I have," I say.

"You care to share?"

"Nice rhyme, geek."

"Punk." He laughs as he says this.

"I chose the side of you and Seppie. I chose the side of friendship."

"Corny! So corny."

"Shut up." I land on the ground and take off instantly again. "You know you love me."

He squeezes a little tighter, holds on a little more, somehow. "I do."

I don't care if he means it romantically or platonically. All I care is that he means it. We are romantic, corny people—no aliens—whatever we are. I hope we never change.

I smile at him and say, "Let's go get an army and rescue Seppie."

CHAPTER 13

When my mom was in the hospital (after we rescued her and after I came back from Washington, D.C., where I had met with China) I had a bit of a nervous breakdown. That isn't a clinical term, but I wasn't diagnosed with anything, so it wouldn't be right to use a clinical term.

Anyway, I just broke one day at school. The world history class was talking about ancient Sumer and its complex language system, which was mirrored by its super-multifaceted religious system that had hundreds of gods and rituals. Every city had a god to protect and guard it. The gods lived with the humans. The humans were the gods' servants.

"Some postulate that the Nephilim from Genesis in the Bible also dwelled here," Mr. Boland said. "They are sometimes thought of as giants, sometimes as fallen angels, sons of God."

Someone got disdainful and said, all disparaging, "You sound like an episode of *Ancient Aliens*."

I tensed.

Mr. Boland raised an eyebrow in that teacher know-it-all way and said, "They have collected clay tablets from Sumer. Do you know what one says? It says that Earth is the seventh planet from the sun. How would they know this? It was around five thousand years ago. Ancient tablets claim that the world was founded by humanlike aliens. They traveled the heavens, used the heavens for their own purposes, claimed the skies and our world as their own. They mined for gold and minerals and decided it was too much work, so they created humans—slaves to do that work for them. They used their own likeness to make us pathetic little creatures."

Grayson Staggs started full-body laughing. Like he was literally convulsing in his seat. Seppie kicked him.

Mr. Boland just kept lecturing. He was used to this. "The first humans couldn't reproduce, so they were tinkered with."

I stood up.

"Ms. Trent. Sit down."

But I couldn't. I couldn't sit down. I took off. The world was too big and too horrible sometimes. I knew everyone just thought this ancient-aliens-in-Sumer thing was an amusing theory, that alien abduction was some silly horror movie plot, but I knew what it was like to be tinkered with, knew how possible the horror actually was. And I couldn't stand it. I still can't stand it.

I ran to the bathroom and hid there, washing my face, trying to calm down.

Seppie found me there by the sinks. She peered at me, hand on my shoulder as I stared down at my freaking shoes, studying them like they held the secret to the universe.

"I know why you freaked out," she said.

I looked up and her eyes were so big and concerned.

"It's because Grayson had spaghetti sauce on his Converse, right? You just couldn't abide the degradation of such awesome shoes?"

I make what I hope is a disgusted face.

"Is it because Lyle's not as good a kisser as you expected? The current slate of presidential candidates is horrible? Is it because the current trending picture of a topless Miley Cyrus has just blown your mind?" she teased. She laughed and poked my cheek with her perfect fingernail. "Ah, there's the famous Mana Trent smile, known to kill hearts throughout New Hampshire's southern counties."

I shook my head. "You're such a dork."

"Why you love me." She announced this and gave me a quick hug from behind. And then she shifted gears, bending so that she could rest her head on my shoulder as we both stared into the disgustingly smudgy bathroom mirror. "We'll find those bastards and get them someday."

"You think?"

"Yeah. I'm with you, Mana, no matter what happens. You know that, right?"

As Lyle, Enoch, and I land on the outskirts of the training camp, I can't forget that conversation. I can't forget how much Seppie meant those words, how she followed me out of class just to make sure that I was okay. That's what friendship is about. It's about love that doesn't have to do with sex. It's about being there for each other, risking everything no matter what.

Lyle hops off my back and puts Enoch on the ground. They both stretch and groan. The sun is rising behind the pine trees. I'm exhausted, but hyped up, too. Enoch pees on a tree.

"Nice," Lyle says.

"She's a dog! You probably pee on trees all the time, don't you?"

"Every chance I get," he counters. His voice loses its teasing tone. "You're hunched over. You okay?"

I straighten up. My back creaks. "Yep. Just a little stiff."

I stare at this place—this camp. This is what I wanted so badly, to be part of this team, to be fighting aliens, saving humanity, and it's not that I don't still want that, but I don't want it this way. I don't want to be involved with anything that Julia Bloomsbury created, anything that didn't trust me enough, anything that made my two best friends lie to me. And right now I want to save Seppie more than I want to save humanity. That might not be right, morally, but she's my priority, not this. If this agency couldn't accept who I am, then they don't deserve my talents or my loyalty. That's that.

Lyle coughs, jolting me out of my thoughts. He looks . . . adorable, rumpled and tall and cute, with those super-big eyebrows and puppy eyes. He clears his throat. "Thanks for the ride. It was faster than me running and carrying you, that's for sure."

"It's nice to be right sometimes." I slap him on the back like we're army buddies or on the football team or something.

He fake-coughs all awkwardly and says, "Easy, killer."

We're standing at the end of a driveway that leads to what I imagine Boy Scout camps would look like. There are log cabins surrounded by trees. A bus and cars rest off to the side. There is a bigger building that's probably some sort of mess hall. A light dusting of snow covers the ground and there are tons of footprints.

"How are we going to convince them to help us?" I ask.

"Motivational speech?"

"Dear God . . ."

He smiles. "I can do that if you want."

"Cool."

"And they know Seppie. They've met her. Seppie is . . ."

"Popular? Awesome? Hot? Well loved?"

"All of the above. I think once they realize she's in jeopardy they'll all be on board."

"Wait. What about the people in charge?"

"That," he sighs, "is the problem. But I was thinking and I might have a plan."

He goes into the building and as I wait for him to come back, I think about him. I can't help it. Lyle is not the type of guy who normally makes a plan, especially the kind with a capital *P*. It isn't that he's dumb. He's brilliant. It's more that he's a spur-of-the-moment type of person, extroverted like Seppie, happiest when he is in the present instead of thinking about the future. He doesn't ignore the future—if he did that he wouldn't have gotten into Dartmouth early decision—but he doesn't dwell on it the way Seppie does, with all her hopes and dreams of a happy life full of academic and professional glory. She wants to be the first black woman president. She would be happy to be the third black woman president, she tells me, because she doesn't want to bring down others' chances for success. Lyle doesn't know what he wants to be, or he didn't know before all this alien stuff happened and he found out he wasn't even human. Me? I dwell on the past, mistakes I've made, happy moments with my mom and/or dad (but mostly my mom), good goofy times with Lyle and Seppie. The future has never been something I wanted to think about and the present usually is just here.

So, when Lyle says that he's going to make the plan, it takes a tiny bit of trust on my part to let him go with this. I remember the Lyle who made the human catapult that was supposed to send me up into the trees, but it only sent me six feet off the ground, backward and into the wading pool. I remember the Lyle who thought that it would be funny to post WHAT DOES IDK MEAN? and then when people responded, I DON'T KNOW, he was all, AGH! WHY DOES NOBODY KNOW WHAT IDK MEANS? That wasn't really a plan, though. Or how once he was trying to mess with Grayson and he Photoshopped pieces of sky out of the picture of the Boston skyline and said, BOSTON TURNS OFF SUNLIGHT FOR LOW-INCOME RESIDENTS. Grayson did not fall for that.

Those are the kinds of plans Lyle is used to creating, not the kind of plan that involves tricking the equivalent of a federal agent so that we can talk to the students that agent is training. Not the kind where you have to lie to a person's face. Not the kind where—

"Hey!" He breaks into my thoughts, all happy-faced and alert. "Done. Let's go."

"What did you do?"

"I pretended I found you and locked you in the panic room, brought them down there, and locked them in. Classic old television show move. Learned it in a million places. Can't believe they fell for it." He's hopping up and down he's so excited. "I feel a bit bad about it because there's no toilet in there. Hopefully nobody needs an early-morning pee or anything."

"Lyle!"

"It's not cool to have to pee in the morning and not be able to."

"Maybe they'll just go on the floor or something?"

"Who knows?"

There are certain things you can't believe you're discussing until you are in the middle of discussing them. This is true at the moment.

"So, we can just go in there and talk to the kids?" I ask, trying not to think about the poor locked-up agents in charge.

"Yep." He's still bouncing on his toes in a happy way. I think he's pretty proud of himself.

"How long do we have to convince them?"

"I would say we have to convince them pretty quickly or risk not convincing them at all."

"No. I meant until the agents get out of the panic room."

"Oh, those guys? They're stuck in there forever until someone pushes the button and lets them out."

Relief fills me.

"That is awesome." I jump up and hug him. "Lyle, you are awesome."

"It's my middle name, Lyle Awesome Stephenson," he kids, but when I let go of him he's got a super-huge smile on his face and I can tell he's stoked. He quickly brushes some hair out of my face, his fingertips just grazing my cheek, and says, "So, let's go."

"Where are they?"

"In the mess hall, waiting for food."

"Cool," I say.

"Cool," he repeats. "We can do this, Mana. I know we can. I'll make everything up to you and we'll get Seppie and we'll all do everything together. Okay?"

For a second I believe it *is* possible. "Okay."

They are all sitting in chairs at tables that are lined up in rows. Nobody looks up when we enter the room, which is all wooden inside, but warm, at least. It's very retro camp, with long logs making up the walls, a giant fire in an immense fireplace at one end. It's toasty and quaint and not exactly how I imagine a training camp for people who fight aliens and the government and, well . . . anything. It's more like a ritzy hotel breakfast room that people who are really white-collar would hang out in to pretend they are deer hunters or something. There are giant bowls of scrambled eggs, hash brown potatoes, platters of sausage, and toast at the center of each table, along with pitchers of orange juice and water. There's a contented buzz of conversation. None of them knows that Lyle's basically kidnapped and abducted their instructors. All of them just think that they are special, handpicked and important, ready to be agents.

This is what I wanted to be. This is why I texted China and hounded him. This is why I felt so heartbroken when that woman denied me what I felt was my freaking birthright. Julia Bloomsbury. I don't even want to think her name.

It seems so sweet and innocent now, so straightforward, to believe in an agency's goodness. Nothing is ever so simple. Isn't that why Mom and China stopped working for the government? It wasn't simple and pure and good. Neither is the agency they work for now, the agency that is training these kids.

There are probably about fifty young adults in here, all happily eating. They look like they range in age from sixteen to thirty. They are all genders and races. It's pretty nice, actually.

"I feel bad for interrupting their breakfast," I whisper to Lyle.

"We're going to need their help."

"I know." I swallow hard. "I feel bad because we're going to put them in danger."

"That's why they are here, Mana. We all have signed up for this."

My nerves flare up. We can never guess at what might be coming, at what we might be leading these people into. And we aren't leaders. We are just kids or young adults or whatever it is fashionable to call us.

"Lyle." I tug at his sleeve.

He's already gearing himself up for a big speech, rubbing his hands together. Both he and Seppie love making speeches. Me? Not so much.

"What is it?"

"I just . . . I want them to know what they are getting into. I want them to have a choice."

He stares at me blankly for a moment. "These are people at an alien-fighting training camp, Mana. Just by being here, they know what they're getting into."

I give a tiny shudder, imagining all the things that could go wrong. Last time, we had to rescue someone (my mother), people died.

"I just don't want to be responsible for their deaths," I admit. "They are . . . They're young . . . And they have moms and dads and dogs, I bet."

Enoch wags her tail.

Lyle does the Shatner, which is a reference we have to the first *Star Trek* captain, actor William Shatner. He played Captain Kirk on television when the series/franchise first began. "The Shatner" means that you face another person and grab them by the sides of their shoulders, sort of cupping that place where the shoulders meet the arms with your hands. You then talk slowly and empathically *and* emphatically. Lyle has not Shatnered me since eighth grade, when he insisted that I shouldn't go to the dance with Nova Levesque because all she wanted to do was feel me up because she had a fetish for Asian girls. Lyle was right. He uses the Shatner sparingly, so I pay attention.

"We are going to use them to rescue Seppie. Seppie has been kidnapped. She is one of them, one of us. They are going to want to save one of their own."

He pauses.

"And?" I ask.

"And you can't feel guilty about it, Mana. Everyone dies. That's just a fact."

"But—"

"There's a possibility that nobody will die. There's a possibility this will be simple."

"But—"

"Yes, there is a possibility that they will, but the moment we sign up for this, we realize that."

"So you and Seppie realized that, too?" I ask. "That means—"

"It means that no matter what else we did with our lives, Dartmouth or MIT or wherever . . . it means that the rest of our lives would be a cover for this. Come on, Mana. You know it, too. There is no better cause, no better life purpose than saving the world and humanity."

"You aren't even human," I whisper.

"Don't remind me." He sighs. "I'm not some self-hating alien, don't get me wrong. But humanity with all its troubles and sicknesses is where I was raised. My heart belongs to it. I'm not going to let you and Seppie and everyone else die because some power-hungry, psychotic aliens want us gone from this world."

I rush into his chest, overcome, and just hug him hard and true. He smells of goodness and snow, cold night air and wool sweaters.

"Please don't lie to me anymore," I say, "even if you're trying to protect me."

"Even if you buy an ugly sweater?" He laughs.

"Even then," I say.

"Deal." His word is a whisper into my hair, soft and husky. And all of a sudden, I want to lean into him even closer, say that I want to know if we've taken a step closer to officially being boyfriend/girlfriend or not. His hand comes up to cup the back of my head and I think he might kiss me. I tilt my head up just in case.

"Ahem. Get a room," someone yells.

I let go and turn around as Lyle clears his throat. Fifty or so future alien hunters stare up at us. Some have their mouths open. Some keep eating. Some have turned around to get a better look.

One particular girl who is built a bit like a wall stands up and roars in a deep throaty voice that reminds me of bullfrogs, "Little Lyley has returned! Who'd you bring, Lyle? Where's Seppie?"

"Lyley?" I whisper.

"Shut up," Lyle mutters back and everyone starts hooting and teasing him. He grimaces. "This is how they show their love."

"Seriously?" I survey the crowd. Many are dressed in those drab-colored T-shirts that you expect the United States military to be wearing. Cargo pants with multiple pockets and dark running shoes are the stand out winners. Their hair is in various states of fashion and there is no uniform buzz-cut thing going on. I guess that's so they don't look too soldiery when they get back home.

"Will you all shut up so I can speak?" Lyle yells. He points at the wall-built girl. "Especially you, Janeice."

I have never heard him say *shut up* before.

Everyone sort of quiets down and Lyle clears his throat again.

Janeice shouts, "You nervous, Lyley? You got your girlfriend here to impress."

"Girlfriend?" I blurt.

"Well . . . yeah . . ." He looks away.

"You told them we were going out?"

"We are."

"We've barely kissed, Lyle." I say this even though inside my heart is doing happy fluttery front tucks in my chest.

"Whatever." He coughs. His cheeks redden. "Not important now, Mana." Raising his voice so that everyone can hear him, he shouts, "Janeice, why don't you shut up and post a biblical quote on Tumblr or something."

"Why don't you go get a prison tattoo?" she shouts back.

"That's not much of a rejoinder," Lyle counters.

"Oh . . . look at Dartmouth and his big words." The guy next to Janeice gives her a high five.

"Are you sure these people like you?" I ask. "It doesn't seem like they like you."

"They're like cops or firefighters. Being mean is how they show their affection," he explains.

"Lovely," I mutter as he clears his throat again.

"People," he begins. "I need your help."

Janeice coughs.

Lyle carries on, "As you know, we have all been recruited here for one thing—to save this world for humankind. We are not here for glory. We are not here for power. We are here for the good of the entire species. And in the last twenty-four hours one of our own has been kidnapped."

There are some gasps. I look at the crowd. Lyle has everyone's attention.

"Seppie has been taken. I was taken, too. And we have reason to believe that Seppie is being held against her will in a facility in Maine. What I'm asking for you guys to do is join us and rescue her. When we came here, we were recruited to make a difference. When we came here, we were recruited to take care of each other and the world. When we came here, we were recruited to put our lives on the line for humanity, so that we could live without enslavement by aliens, so we could live on a planet that was safe. When we go up there to rescue Seppie, we aren't just rescuing Seppie; we are giving each other hope. This is our first battle, people, and it's a battle for one person, because one person matters. Every human being matters." He pauses, looks around. "Will you help us?"

Lyle's speech is actually pretty good and everyone is quickly on board, which seems both magical and amazing to me. Then they start hammering out questions about what is going on, and who I am exactly, and whether or not I can be 100 percent sure where Seppie is.

It is obvious to me that I need to pull out the crystal again even though I don't want to. The alien girl said not to trust anyone. She said . . . But trust is important. Trust allows us to have relationships, to work together, to save the world.

"Guys, okay . . ." I use my loudest, most commanding voice. "I have something to show you. But we can't talk about it outside of this room, okay?"

Janeice goes downstairs to feed the counselors locked in the room since they are going to be in there for a while, and the rest of us close all the doors and windows. This is a big deal for me, showing them this, but how can I expect them to help me save Seppie if I don't give them the whole truth? This crystal, whatever it is, is part of the whole truth.

"It will be fine," says a guy with slightly pointy ears and a frowning face. He smells like sausage. "We're all right here with you."

I appreciate that he's trying to be nurturing even though we just met. Lyle rolls his eyes because I guess he might be having a jealous Lyle moment. I also appreciate this. But I push it all out of my head as I touch the crystal and think about Seppie.

"Show me Seppie," I whisper and let it go. "This is how we knew she was at the YMCA in Bar Harbor."

The crystal whirls away from me and into the center of the room. There are a couple of appreciative gasps, but not too many. These soon-to-be soldiers are used to weird stuff already, I guess.

The crystal flickers around and shows us woods. Lots of woods. Snow covers the ground between the trees, which are mostly pine and thick with boughs. There's a dark building that's built into the ground.

"That's not the Mount Desert Island YMCA located on Park Street in Bar Harbor, Maine, across from the ball field," Lyle says, sounding a bit like the automated voice on a GPS mapping app. "It looks nothing like the YMCA building we saw before."

"It's probably near the original location," a girl named Abony says. Her dark hair is pulled back in a no-nonsense ponytail and she commands all four feet five inches of her body with the confidence of an athlete. She should cheer. "They've obviously moved her."

Moving closer to the projection that covers the central dining room tables, I try to glean something: some detail, some characteristic.

"It's on a hill," I say. "It's . . . There are trees everywhere."

Nobody says *duh,* but they should.

I point to the right-hand edge of the image. In the distance, something reflects light. The green is more man-made than natural. "Over there."

The crystal zooms in. There's a street sign. Spring Street.

"Seppie," I whisper. "Where are you?"

"Someone check and see if there is a Spring Street in Bar Harbor, Maine," Lyle orders. I'm impressed by this new take-action, give-orders Lyle. I side-eye him. His profile is looking strong.

"There is!" Abony says, pretty triumphantly. "It's right near that Y, too, less than a mile away."

"Bingo!" Lyle gives me a fist bump and then slaps everyone nearby. "Road trip?"

People start clamoring and getting all excited, but I'm all like, "It isn't showing me Seppie. I can't actually see Seppie in there. Why is that?"

I move directly beneath the crystal as everyone else starts gathering supplies and shouting orders.

"Where is Seppie?" I demand.

The crystal whirls and shows me the front of the building and then comes back. It shows the front door and then pulls back.

I'm still demanding a real image of Seppie, the actual person, as Lyle starts barking orders and plans about our attack. Abony has pulled up the Google Earth application on her computer so that they can scout out the layout of the compound and the land. It's definitely a hill, someone says. There is a blur on the top of the Google Earth picture, though, like it's hiding something. We zoom out and check the area: little mountains; mostly straight roads in the small town of Bar Harbor, then curving, federal government–owned roads that run through the nearby national park. I appreciate all that, but I'm still confused. Why isn't it showing me Seppie? How do we even know she's there? Snatching the crystal out of the air, I resist the urge to throw it against the wall. Every time I use it, it feels like a piece of me goes missing, like someone is seeing me the way I am seeing them. But this time? This time it feels the worst—like doom and destruction. I feel like I'm being used by the crystal just as much as I am using *it*.

Enoch rubs her nose against my shin and I crouch down while I pocket the crystal. "What is it, honey? Are you hungry? Thirsty?"

She wags her tail and we make our way toward the kitchen area, which is separated from the dining room by a long counter. There are vast yellow tubs of sugar in the open wooden cabinets. A plate of bacon, cooked but uneaten, rests on the counter. I figure this is safe for dogs and drop her a couple of pieces. She wags her tail enthusiastically as some of the trainees scurry about, packing supplies into coolers.

"We're only going to Maine," I say.

Sausage guy has a giant tub of pancake batter. "It's best to be prepared."

Another guy, Noah, hauls a crate of bottled water out from under a counter and heads out the back door, reminding me that dogs need water and bacon is so salty that even if Enoch hadn't been thirsty before, she should be now. I find a metal mixing bowl, fill it with water, and place it on the floor for her, squatting down to pet her as she laps it up.

"What do you think? You trust them?" comes a whisper from behind the counter.

"It's Lyle, man. How do you not trust Lyle?"

"He's an alien. And the girl? Who even is she?"

"Nobody. Just his girlfriend and Seppie's best friend."

Enoch stops drinking and looks up at me. The voices move away, but it's too late. I've heard them.

"Should we tell them?" I whisper. It doesn't feel fair that they don't know what I can do. I mean, we trusted them about the crystal, shouldn't we trust them about what I am? Who I am? I'm not a *what*, no matter what was done to me. I am a *who*.

Enoch shakes her head and I think if dogs could speak English she'd be telling me, "Not yet."

*E*noch's lack of total trust worries me, so when everyone is piling into a giant yellow school bus, I corner Lyle. We're away from everyone so that they can't hear.

"You think we can trust them?" I ask.

"Yeah." He gives a wave to a guy with a crew cut, the most military looking out of all of them. Mason.

"Then how come you haven't told them about me?" My hands go to my hips.

"That's your story to tell. Not mine," he says.

I eye him after that comment because he sounds like his mother, like he has thought this through well and hard. The world is quiet except for the racket of the others heading onto the bus. I'm not even sure what to call them. Soldiers? Agents? Young adults? Kids?

Students? *People* is the only word that doesn't come across like a label, but it fails to be specific enough. I sigh. *Futures.* That's what Lyle called them. I wonder if that's because the future depends on them or because they are future agents. Either way works, I guess.

"I want everyone to be okay," I say. "I mean, they are all risking a lot for one person, even if it is Seppie."

"It's a no-man-left-behind kind of world, Mana, or at least it should be. You can't abandon your friend to—"

"Even if it means risking others?"

"You don't want to save Seppie?"

"Of course I do!" I am almost shouting. Enoch growls in confusion. Lyle scratches her butt. This calms her down and it somehow calms me down, too. "You know that you and Seppie are my people, my no-man-left-behinds, but I worry that we're risking other people who are loved, who are needed."

"They are making their own choices. I thought we already went through the moral-questioning phase of this. Why are you circling back?"

"I know . . . I know . . ." I try to wave the thoughts away. "It just isn't easy and simple. It's not all black-and-white polarities, you know."

"It never is."

"It is in a basketball game. You have your home team and you root for it."

He nods, gazes at the earth, opens his arms up wide like he's calling it all to him. "How about your team is Team Earth."

"And Team Earth consists of?"

"Anyone who wants to save humanity without genocide of aliens or any other species."

"That works."

He pulls me into a hug, smooshing Enoch in between us. "Thought it would. Now let's go find September."

CHAPTER 14

The drive to Maine is bumpy in a school bus, but I take the first two hours of the five-hour trip as a time to sleep, slumped against Lyle's shoulder. Enoch has made friends with pretty much everyone on the bus except for Rebecca (allergic to dogs) and Stephanie (afraid of dogs) and a guy named Kyle who doesn't like dogs and therefore is untrustworthy, because honestly, who doesn't like dogs? Only the untrustworthy.

I wake up sort of refreshed and with a big spot of dog drool on my leg. Enoch has climbed onto our laps while I slept and her doggy jowls have left a wet spot. Driving the bus in front of us is Janeice, whose mom is a bus driver in Lincoln, Nebraska, which seems terribly far away. This somehow qualifies Janeice to drive the bus.

"Winter is worse there," she tells us. "I've never been to Maine, but they've got hardly any snow compared to home."

"It's because they're on the coast," Lyle says. "The sea keeps the temperature a bit warmer."

"Mr. Meteorologist, Lyley Lyle." Janeice is not easy to like, but I'm not picky. She's here. She's transporting us. That's all that matters.

"I thought only I was allowed to call you Lyley Lyle. Me and Seppie," I whisper.

"She doesn't do it out of love and friendship." He yawns, stretching his arms up and touching the roof.

"Obviously."

"Not like you do."

I harrumph.

"You admitted last night that you love me."

I make a nice, noncommittal noise.

"Oh, hold on . . . let me guess . . . You're going to do the whole 'maybe I said it, maybe I didn't' approach or maybe the Mana patented 'I love everyone, what is the big deal' approach or maybe the—"

"Do you want me to *love you* love you? Is that what you're saying?" I interrupt, amused.

"Dear God," Janeice blurts from the driver's seat. "This is pathetic."

"I'm not saying that," Lyle starts. Enoch jumps up and walks to the back of the bus.

"What are you saying, then?" I ask.

He groans and hits the side of his head against the bus window. "You can't just make it easy on me, can you?"

"Never."

My phone buzzes. Janeice has been charging it up. She hands it back to me while everyone shouts, "Eyes on the road, Janeice!"

I take the phone from her backward-extended arm. It's a message from China. I suck in my breath.

"What's it say?" Lyle asks.

"It says, WHERE ARE YOU?" I read.

"Don't tell him," Lyle suggests.

I text back, WHERE I AM WANTED.

"Harsh," Lyle says in a sort of appreciative way. I am glad he enjoys my passive-aggressive snark.

The phone rings. I stare at it.

People start chanting for me to answer it. I let it ring and go to voice mail, which is really sort of conflict-averse of me. Also, it's sort of payback for those weeks China ghosted me.

He immediately texts me, ANSWER YOUR PHONE.

I LEFT BECAUSE YOUR BOSS WANTS ME DEAD.

SAYS WHO? he texts back.

"Are you sure you want to go there?" Lyle says.

"I can't tell him who," I admit, "because I don't want Jon to get hurt. I just won't answer. Should I tell him we're rescuing Seppie?"

ARE YOU WITH THE FUTURES? China's text comes through despite my lack of an answer.

"What should I say?" I ask.

"Yes," Lyle and Janeice and Sausage Guy, whose name is Will, all say.

YES, I text.

The phone rings again. I silence it.

"Wimping out," Janeice announces.

"You know when you come home drunk after curfew? And your mom is standing there at the door? It's like that, not that I've done that," I say. "It isn't that I'm especially conflict-averse or anything even though . . . yeah . . . I don't know . . . I just don't have the energy to deal with it right now." I shut off the phone. I'm such a mess that I can't even be self-aware enough to determine if I'm conflict-averse or not. "He'll figure it all out soon enough. That's what he does."

I turn the phone back on.

"What are you doing?" Lyle asks.

"I forgot to tell him to let out the counselors," I say as I text China the info. "I'm sure they must need to pee by now. I don't want them locked in there forever."

"She really is too nice," Janeice says.

"I know," Lyle says.

They all say it like it's a character flaw. Lyle says it like he isn't too nice, too.

We don't stop until we hit a gas station/Fuddruckers/Tim Hortons combination place in Ellsworth, Maine, and we only stop there because of the lovely combination of burger, coffee, doughnuts, and milk shakes. And the bathroom. We make lines at the bathroom and then all fill up on take-out food. Enoch stays in the bus because dogs aren't allowed. I miss her and buy her a burger because that seems like the most canine-friendly choice.

I have to admit that I don't notice when the door opens.

"Everyone down!" someone orders.

That's when I notice them. Two men, black suits, sunglasses, hats, guns. They could be clones, but one has a freckle on his left cheek and a half of an inch on the other guy. They notice me noticing them.

"She's here," the taller one announces, moving forward.

"Ah, hell to the no," Abony says, moving forward to block him. He backhands her, but she keeps coming until his elbow connects with her face.

A huge noise shakes the entire restaurant. The woman behind the counter has shot the ceiling. Pieces of drywall scatter down around some knitting she's been working on. Janeice tucks me behind her, a wall of protection. I push my way back out.

"Nobody is taking anybody," the cashier announces.

Abony, rubbing at her cheek, says, "I like her."

The shorter man in black aims his weapon at the woman behind the counter. Her glasses are perched at the end of her nose. She doesn't back down one bit. "I'm an off-duty police officer and my husband owns this establishment. I suggest you drop your weapons, lay down on the floor, and put your hands behind your backs like good little boys."

"I *really* like her," Janeice says, but the Men in Black do not comply.

One jumps forward, shoots toward the off-duty cop, and seems to clip her shoulder. The other one lunges toward Janeice and me. Noah smashes him with a direct roundhouse kick to the face. The Man in Black somehow remains standing. Another shot roars through the building and the first Man in Black falls to the ground. Then it's a mess of movement, frenzied chaos. Lyle's yanking me backward. The other Man in Black is shooting toward the officer and then trying to bash Janeice out of his way. A huge throng of Futures swarm him. Something bangs. And he's down. Janeice has her leg square on his back, and a guy whose name I don't remember has taken his weapon and is tying his hands.

"You okay? Mana, you okay?" Lyle shakes me.

"Yeah . . . just . . . the lady?" I push through the crowd and get to the off-duty officer. The owl hat she'd been knitting is stained with blood. Her shoulder bleeds onto her shirt.

"Just a graze," she says, but her teeth grit right after she speaks.

Grabbing paper towels off the counter, I press them into her shoulder. "Keep your shoulder elevated, okay? Stay sitting up. Don't bend," I say. "You were super-brave. Anyone call nine-one-one?"

Abony announces she has.

I touch the lady officer's face and move the owl away, then beckon one of the few patrons who are not with us over to me. I show her what to do. She's wearing a University of Maine sweatshirt and perspiring because she's so nervous and shaky. I put her hands on top of the paper towels, which have already soaked through. I think better of this, grab a latex glove from the box on the counter, and get the glove on the shaking woman's hand. Then we try again.

"Apply pressure," I tell her, trying to remember everything I learned in that wilderness first aid class I took back in seventh grade. "Make sure that—I don't know your name—"

"Katia," the off-duty cop says.

"Make sure that Katia stays awake until the ambulance gets here, okay?" I say.

The other Futures have bundled up and restrained both Men in Black. One appears to be dead. They've restrained him anyway.

"Thank you," I say to Katia.

"Where are you going? You kids are witnesses," she says.

"We have to save someone," I say. "We can't stay. I'm so sorry. Thank you again." I turn my attention to the shaking lady in the University of Maine sweatshirt. "You can do this. Just apply pressure for a bit, keep her talking. You be a hero like her, okay?"

Her voice trembles and she's saying, "Okay," even as Lyle is yanking me toward the front door.

We all assemble outside the bus. Sirens wail in the distance. We don't have much time. We have to get going before the cops arrive, but Abony and Noah have been inspecting the bus. Abony grabs a small black device from the wheel well. Enoch is barking like mad, trying to get out.

"This," Abony announces, "is how they were tracking us."

"It wasn't there before," Noah says. "I checked that wheel before we left."

Nobody says the obvious. Nobody says that one of us must have put it there. We all just stare at each other. I call Enoch out of the bus.

"Abony, have her sniff it," I suggest.

Abony extends her arm to Enoch, who trots right over and takes a good whiff of the tracking device.

"Enoch, tell us who else has touched—"

Before I can even stop talking, Enoch has trotted over to Will and barks. Sausage guy? Seriously? Will lifts up his hands. Enoch barks again.

"Will?" Mason's face is stunned. They sat together on the bus. They are probably bros.

"Dog is wrong, man. Not me," Will insists.

Everyone just sort of stands there. It's not like we have magic lie-detector serum or anything on us, but I'm sure Enoch is right.

"Let's just tie him up so that we don't have to worry about him. We'll figure it all out later," I suggest and everyone agrees after a bit of discussion. Abony and Mason do most of the work with the restraints and they put Will right in the middle of the bus, so that everyone can keep an eye on him and he's not too close to any exits. He protests, but not too much. I guess he's smart enough to realize it would be a waste of time. Lyle and Janeice talk about how disappointed they are about this, but I figure when you have this many people, you can't count on being able to trust them all 100 percent. We haven't been together long enough to be completely certain about each other. It's more of a blow to everyone else, probably, than to me, because they trained with Will a bit. The agency is supposed to put everyone through tests to make sure that they are trustworthy and their allegiances are correct. It just somehow failed with Will. Or did it?

"Will," I ask once we're all on the bus and heading to Bar Harbor again, finally, "who did you put that tracking device on there for? Was it for the Men in Black?"

He shakes his head. "No."

Everyone starts listening.

"Who, then?" Abony demands. She's pretty annoyed.

"The agency. We're supposed to be working for them, remember? Not these two."

"The agency wanted to kill Mana!" Lyle protests.

"Well, maybe they were right." Will is unapologetic. "They know more than we do about what's going on and they especially know more than we do about her."

I glare at him and resist the urge to call him a name, because my mom taught me to be polite. "Your tracking device was hijacked by the Men in Black. It brought them right to us. Who knows who else it's going to attract?" I ask.

"Well, it's in a Dumpster at Fuddruckers now," he says with a shrug. "No loss."

"People were hurt back there!" I lift my hands to the ceiling. I do not like Will Who Smells Like Sausage. I do not like him at all.

Noah smacks Will on the back of the head. Lyle grabs his hand. "We're better than that."

Noah smirks. "Hardly."

"I'm just saying that you all are trusting these two over the agency, over your training," Will announces. "Think about that. I'm the only one actually following protocol here."

Abony slaps duct tape over his mouth. "I vote we silence Will. Everyone with me?"

Nobody objects. His words sting, though. He is sort of right. Abony must notice my sadness because she slings an arm over my shoulder as we stand there in the bus aisle.

"The agency is not about friendship. The agency is about rules," she says. "We all love Seppie. We're going to make sure she's safe. Right, guys? It's not that we're abandoning our training, we're just using it to help one of our own. Am I right?"

"Right."

"Right."

"Damn freaking straight."

"She's too hot to lose."

Abony rolls her eyes. I agree.

"Absolutely," some other guy says.

"For Seppie!" This last yell is Janeice, who then follows up with, "You all better sit down. It looks like we have a bumpy road ahead."

CHAPTER 15

It takes us all a few minutes to calm down. Well, Janeice and Mason are pretty fine and happily eating their burgers (Janeice drives and eats, which is pretty spectacular), but the rest of us are silent, and then babbling, and then just sort of processing everything that's happened. Will keeps trying to give everyone the stanky eye, but Abony threatens to cover his eyes with duct tape and he starts just gazing out the window instead.

"You worried?" Lyle asks.

"Absolutely," I tell him. Enoch puts her head on my knee. I sort of absentmindedly pet her head. We have driven over a small two-lane road, veered left, and followed the perimeter road around Mount Desert Island toward Bar Harbor. To the left of the bus is a bay and the mainland, to our right is woods and mini-mountains covered in snow. I shiver. "I am absolutely worried."

"Me, too. But we'll get Seppie. It will be okay."

"How do you know?"

"There's no other choice," he says.

About fifteen minutes later we roll through Bar Harbor proper, which is mostly a ghost town with restaurants and tourist shops boarded up. There are signs everywhere that say SEE YOU NEXT SEASON or THANK YOU FOR YOUR PATRONAGE. BE BACK IN MAY. Pretty much the only things that appear open are the Hannaford, a grocery store with a parking lot that can maybe fit fifty cars, and an Art Deco theater called the Criterion, which has a benefit for David Bridges as the announcement on its marquee. I wonder who David Bridges is and hope he'll be okay.

"Almost there," Janeice announces as we head three blocks out of the main part of town and toward the YMCA. The Y seems the most logical and least conspicuous place to park a school bus other than an actual school, and the closest one of those is miles away. Once we've parked, we split up into groups of five, heading out toward the compound that we saw in the crystal. It is surrounded by three rural streets: Spring, Cromwell Harbor Road, and Kebo. Lyle and I head with three others to the Spring Street side. When we get there, we see woods, a hill with granite outcroppings, and a bunker deep in the woods.

The bunker is very World War II Nazi cliché, dark concrete walls hidden in a dark forest. Men and women in black clothes and bulletproof vests range around the perimeter. They have assault rifles in their hands—American, not alien, guns.

"She is in here?" I ask Lyle because for some illogical reason, I'm overwhelmed with self doubt. "You're sure? I mean. We aren't making a mistake are we? We all saw this, right? This is—"

"This has to be it." He bites at the edge of his lip.

Our team is bizarre-looking. The Futures' clothes are a hodge-podge of fatigues and punk rock, American Eagle preppy and hunter camo. But they all have steely gazes and look as ready as they can be.

"This is going to be the second time I have to rescue her," I announce.

"My turn next?" he quips.

"Don't even." I fist-bump him. He fist-bumps me back. And then I climb on his back. The plan is to have everyone create a diversion on the right flank of the building. Then, Lyle will run in with his super-speed, which doesn't quite merit superhero status but is pretty damn fast—faster than a human—and I will fend off any attackers with my sonic boom or whatever the hell it is that happens when I drink caffeine.

"Got the Coke?" I ask.

"Root beer."

"Lyle!"

"It's the kind with real sugar and not corn syrup, and it's full of caffeine. Not all root beer is created equal. It's time you got to taste the caffeine kind."

"That is sweet of you."

He becomes all big-eyed. "Sweet of me! Get it? Sugar? Sweet?"

"Lyle, I get it. I'm the one who said it."

He just laughs and passes me the plastic bottle of root beer. I gulp it down.

"Not too much, Mana!"

"I want to be sure." My heart is already racing so fast. I pass the bottle back down and as Lyle replaces the cap, I press my hand to my chest.

"How does it feel?" he asks.

"Like my heart is going to explode," I admit, trying to sound cocky and not terrified. "So, perfect."

I give him a noogie on the top of his head just as shouting starts. There is an explosion to the right, deep in the woods, but the smoke is visible, hurling dark and green toward the sky.

"Now?" he asks.

"Now." I tighten my legs around his back as he leans forward and starts to run, darting between the trees. A good two-thirds of the people milling around protecting the front entrance have rushed off to the right, toward the explosion and our diversion, but there are still another third here, protecting the entrance.

Behind us run the rest of our troops, the infiltration team, but they can't keep up with Lyle when he runs. Nobody can. Well, maybe me with my flying/bounding thing, but that's not what's happening here. Others will approach or are approaching from the other streets.

We push forward, fast and swift and not human, so far from

human. My cells electrify, power courses through them, and this feeling? At first it was scary, this power—but it's also good to feel so alive, to feel like I have some sort of purpose or meaning or something. And it feels good to be part of a group of beings who all have the same goal.

We howl silently through that frozen forest. We rage inside ourselves as we run; we scream. We are soldiers—some of us older, some of us younger; some of us brand-new at this, some of us who have seen violence before—but when we run, the motion of our need propels us forward, focuses us, makes us zero in on the raw nature of who we are and what we want; yes, we want to save our friend, but more than that, we want to survive.

We move through the trees, behind the boulders, separating on the frozen, broken earth. We cling to our orders—distract, for most of us; defend, for others; attack, for Lyle and me, as we're the ones with the closest ties to Seppie. We bring with us our need for closure, for questions to be answered, and for our friend to be with us again, safe. She has to be safe or else this is all pointless. We leave behind our worries as we rush through the patient, long-standing woods. We triumph in our approach. Almost there. *Almost there.* Guns sound to our left. Screams pierce the air to our right.

"Hold on," Lyle says.

We blast into the open space in front of the bunker. A head-on assault seems foolhardy, ignorant, and pretty egotistical, which is why everyone voted in favor of it when we had our tactics discussion on the bus. And the noises put the remaining guards on alert. They stare with focused eyes and raise their guns.

"Lyle!" I scream as he keeps rushing forward, straight at them. I yank him up and backward as they shoot, pulling us into a huge, double-person back handspring. The bullets fly and something hits my arm, but I almost don't feel it, I'm so full of power and rage. We land a few feet backward and the men are there, raising their guns again.

This time it's Lyle who screams *my* name and I lift my hand, focusing. The energy whooshes out almost like a shock wave. Bullets stop and drop to the snow. The guards topple backward. We run forward to the door, which has a keypad.

"Did you kill them?" Lyle asks.

"I don't know." I touch the keypad, focusing, breathing hard. Numbers fly through my head as I try to descramble the entry code before the guards come alive again (if they are still alive) or their reinforcements come. The code . . . the code . . .

*2754*76*

I hit the sequence that rushes through my head.

She comes.

"There's a voice in my head," I tell Lyle. "Male."

"Is that how you got the code?"

"I don't know."

"It could be a trap, Mana. This could all be a trap." His eyes are wide and panicked, and for some reason his panic makes me more confident. We have been through a lot, Lyle and Seppie and me. No matter how often we mess up, we will always love each other and have each other's back. So, now . . . now that he's panicked, I will be strong for him and for her.

I say as calmly as I can, "I know that. You know that. It's obvious."

He shakes his head. "I didn't really know that."

"Sweetie, you're supposed to be the smart one. I think you knew it, deep inside." A tiny bit of my anger peels away as I go up on tiptoe and kiss his cheek right before I kick the door open to reveal a hallway that branches into two different corridors. The walls are sterile, metal and concrete. Like a hospital wing in a poor hospital. Like a bunker.

We scurry down the hallway, sticking to the sides, and then it opens into a huge room, big and dark and full of staircases that resemble fire escapes, connecting one level of catwalk to another. Behind those catwalks are other rooms and two more hallways. At the lowest level are cars of all types and value, Kias and Subarus and Ford trucks and Lexuses. Guns line the walls, set in racks. I stare past the weapons and at the enormity of the space.

"This place is huge," I whisper. "We'll have to split up."

"I don't want to split up."

"We have to. We'll never get through it fast enough."

"You're never supposed to split up. It never goes well! I could cite a million times in movies and TV shows where that—"

I kiss him full on the lips. They are rigid beneath mine, but after a split second they yield to softness. I've shocked him. Good. That was my point. I break away. "Be fast then, Lyle. Be fast and safe."

"You, too! No heroics."

"Of course not." I give a cocky smile that is still totally the opposite of how I'm feeling. He rushes right and I move left. Seppie could be in any of these cars, tucked in a trunk, smooshed into a backseat, but it doesn't feel right. I decide to save the bottom floor to search last, and instead head up to the rooms off the first catwalk. I search room after room. They're all bunks and sleeping areas on this level. Men sleeping. There is a man peeing. I lock him in his room.

An alarm goes off, and thundering footsteps immediately sound below and above me. I bypass the stairs, pulling myself up onto the lower level of a catwalk as men run beneath me. None of them looks up. People never look up. As soon as they pass, I swing myself up to the next level, praying that Lyle is being careful, praying that one of us will find Seppie soon.

I try to focus, like I can feel Seppie somehow, but that's silly. I do, however, get a gut reaction: to go up to the fourth level. I listen to it. I sneak and run and crawl and scurry up three more metal staircases, trying to be invisible, and then I get to the fourth level, where I run smack into a woman with angry eyes and principal hair. She's got a gun. Of course she does. Everyone has a gun; it's the United States.

"Have you come for your friend?" She smiles. Her mouth is full of blood. "You're too late."

That's when I recognize her.

"Mrs. Sweet?" I may actually gasp.

"So shocked. You never were the brightest student, were you, Mana? Not compared to Lyle or Seppie."

Wow. Seriously? Could people stop talking about my supposed lack of intelligence eventually?

"The world isn't about being the best at taking tests and memorizing information," I counter, looking for a way to get by her. She has a gun pointed at me, but she's sort of casual about it, like pointing a gun at a student is just an everyday sort of thing. No big.

"Oh, really?" Her smile drips sarcasm. "What's it about, then? Friendship? Loyalty?"

"Sometimes." I shrug. "Sometimes it's about kicking butt and taking names. Sometimes it's about passing your world history test. Sometimes it's about finally having a reason to knock your pain-in-the-butt school principal unconscious and not have to worry about getting suspended and having it on your permanent record."

She laughs. "So much bravado, Mana. Yet, I see you're still talking." She moves closer with the gun so that it's within my reach. "Let's get going."

"Where?"

"Time to take you to my leader."

"You've always wanted to say that, haven't you?" I quip, just to get her off her game.

"Always."

The gun is in my face and I hope for the best, trying to channel everything Seppie taught me about gun defense, which she allegedly had just started to learn at those Krav Maga classes that she was allegedly taking. I know that's a lie now. It doesn't matter. The first rule is to redirect where the gun will hit, the next is to control the weapon, the third is to counterattack.

So I smack my arm down on top of Mrs. Sweet, pushing her gun arm toward the ground, and clamp my hand on the inside of her wrist—which is larger than I imagined, and my hands are small. I move my other hand down along her arm as fast as I can until it touches the barrel and then I slant forward. The gun fires. It misses me, but my ears ring from the noise of it and I grunt, grabbing the gun.

"Where's your super-alien powers?" she snarls at me through her gritted teeth. I yank the gun out of her hand and point it at her.

"Don't need them."

"Life would have been so much easier if you just went home when you were pretending to be sick at school."

"Why is that?"

"We had an ambush waiting for you there. Then we had an ex-terminator follow you to the woods. You left. Then it followed you to the hospital. You all killed it. It's been such a ridiculous forty-eight hours. And it's your fault. I'm tired of the chase." She raises an eyebrow. "You'll have to shoot me."

I shrug like that's no big deal. She lunges toward me, but I flip up and away, down a hallway. I slam the door shut behind me, triumphant. I lock it and hope she doesn't know the code. She probably does.

This hallway is whiter than the others, like it's less used. I run down it. She's banging on the door behind me, calling for help. Lovely. I need to hurry. I give up all hope of not being detected in here.

Honestly, though, I'm not the best fighter. I haven't been trained to fight. I kind of suck at it and my hands hurt from just that gun defense.

"Seppie!" I yell and then do it again. "September!"

I listen.

Nothing.

I slam open a door. A medical room of some sort? There is a hospital bed. Restraints. But no Seppie.

But this is it . . . This was the room I kept seeing . . . the room with the man with dark hair. Panic fills me. What have they done to her?

I barge out into the hallway. There is more noise at the door. Banging. So much banging. I don't have much time and I don't want to use my power again because I honestly don't know how to actually control it. I don't know if I'll run out of juice. I know nothing. Nothing.

I hate knowing nothing. I pause and take a sip of root beer, just in case I need to recharge. The buzz of the caffeine seeps through me. I can do this. Moving faster now, I yell Seppie's name, throwing open every door that I come to. It's the eighth one that I come to. That's when I find her.

Seppie is alone in a dark room. Sunlight barely slants through a window full of bars. She's strapped onto a table, fully clothed—thank god, because I did not want to take her out of here naked. She would hate that. Plus, it's cold. Her eyes stare up at the ceiling and she's mumbling numbers that don't make any sense to me.

Rushing to her, I start unbuckling the straps holding her down. It takes too long. I rip them off her instead. The caffeine has definitely made me stronger.

"Seppie? September?" I tap her face.

Her eyes focus. "Mana?"

"You're alive."

"You're . . . observant?" She gives a faint little smile.

I wrap my arm around her waist and heave her off the table. "Can you walk? We have to go. We're attacking the base but—"

"We?"

"Me. Lyle. Some people we recruited. Well, Lyle recruited. Your camp friends or pretend Krav Maga friends or something . . . I don't know. The future agents. The Futures. That's what you call yourselves, right?" I tighten my hold on her as I steer her out of the room and back into the corridor. There are shouts to the left, so I peel back toward the right and the door that the principal is still trying to break through.

"No," she says. "The left is the way out. It's . . . yeah . . ."

Her voice breaks my heart—there is so much weakness in it.

"What did they do to you? Who are these people?" I ask, even though I'm not sure I want to know.

"They—I think—I think they were trying to get you. They did experiments?"

"Aliens?"

"No. People. Definitely people. Except one. One is like you, I think." She pushes off my arm and hobbles next to me. "I'm not much of a pacifist anymore. Just so you know. So if you see this guy, you have my permission to kill him."

"Good to know. I'm not much of a pacifist anymore either," I admit and hurry down the corridor, checking to make sure she's behind me. Her back is a little bent like she's in pain—a lot of pain—but she keeps up.

"There are stairs . . . to the right . . ."

We clang down iron stairs, our feet making so much noise. Below us is grass, but it's a couple of stories down. Smoke from small fires ripples through the air. I have no idea what has been happening out here, but my heart worries for Lyle and the others. The stairs give the impression of forming a U shape of platforms around what might be a garage for super-tall cars. Each landing wraps around and is bordered by pipes and fences so you don't fall out. It's very industrial feeling, grimy and dark. This place is so huge. We didn't know what we were getting into. I pray for the others, for Lyle, for us, for the dozens of stories of fighting that are going on right here, right now, stories that are so close to me but I will never know. So many people and so many lives and dramas and needs. All right here. Struggling to win. It makes me dizzy to think of it.

"Your arm is bleeding," Seppie announces.

"I got shot. I think it's a graze or something."

She freaks out.

"It's fine."

"It's so not fine," she whispers.

"Honestly, it hurt more to do gun defenses with Mrs. Sweet."

Her mouth drops open in shock.

"I should have practiced more with you."

"I told you."

We're only half a flight down when a voice rings through the building. "Oh. Little Mana. How lovely! I'm so glad you joined us."

A man stands all the way across the giant room, standing on another platform, smiling and slightly smudged, but obviously not worried about his safety, not considering me a threat.

Which means . . .

Which means . . .

He's not a good guy. Shock ripples through me. I trusted him. I worried about him. He played me?

"Wharff?" I don't move. China's quick guide to situational awareness runs through my head. What did he say? The first sign of danger, you should run. But where? Up the stairs? Down? The second option is to hide. Again, where? The third option is to fight. But the enemy and his little principal BFF are across the landings, so far away. I'm not sure if my sonic-boom thing can work that far.

I go four more steps down to the catwalk and then lean against the railing, super-casual, as if I'm unworried. Seppie follows me, still not standing upright all that well.

Wharff leans against the railing on his side, just as casual, mirroring my posture. "It's good to meet you again. I knew your caring heart would bring you here." He indicates the smoke and fire and bedlam beneath us. "I didn't quite count on you bringing so much backup, but . . ." He winks. "It makes it more fun, doesn't it?"

"This is bad," Seppie says. "This is tremendously bad. Do you know him?"

"We've met," he answers for me, and suddenly the distance feels too close. To be fair, a hundred miles would be too close.

He was the person the crystal showed me a few times—at least it was the back of the head. I can tell now even though he's facing me. That was him. Why?

Finally, I fight through the shock and find my voice. "So, I'm guessing you weren't driving a truck on a highway in Maine and didn't have a happy abduction story?"

"Hardly." He raises an eyebrow. It's a calculated move and is meant to make me worry about how casual he is. "There are no happy abduction stories. You two should know that. But to be fair, we tried to be as noninvasive as possible with your friend September here."

I whirl around. "What did they do to you?"

Something zings through the air behind me and I smash down to the grate, yanking September with me.

"Lesson one is to never turn your back on an enemy, Mana," he calls from across the hangar/garage/whatever the hell this is.

I lift up my head. "So you're the enemy?"

"He kidnapped me and shot a freaking dart at us," September grumbles. "I'd say he's the enemy. We need to get out of here."

"One sec." I stand up even though I know it makes me a bigger target, but if September is right and it was a dart he shot at us, it seems he doesn't want me dead. He wants me weak and docile and captured, but not dead. At least not yet. I bellow across the room, "What do you want from me?"

"Everything. Nothing."

"That's no answer."

"Your power. I want your power."

"To do what?"

"To fight the aliens." Mrs. Sweet is the one who answers this time and she is wearing her patented You Are Not a Worthy Student look. She must have been the one to clean up the dead bodies in the bathroom. She must have been trying to get to the crystal but it was too late. She glares at me.

"Shouldn't that make us friends?" I ask. "We're on the same side. My friends and I like to call it Team Earth."

Seppie mumbles something, but I don't hear her, which is probably good. Seppie hates cute code names. Mrs. Sweet coughs and mumbles something, but I can't hear what she says.

"I know it's not the best name," I babble, "but it's a pretty descriptive one. It means we are in favor of continuing the human population of earth without any genocidal destruction of alien or human species. You like it?"

Wharff eyes me. "Do you have the crystal?"

"What crystal?" I hedge.

"The crystal that shows where the rest of us are."

"What do you mean, 'rest of us'?" I ask.

"The Enhanced."

Seppie leans up toward me. "Mana, this is all a trap to get you and get the crystal. Mostly the crystal. Whatever the crystal is. Is it like the chip thing?"

"I know," I mumble back to her. "I mean, I know now. I mean, I know now about the trap part."

Another dart flies through the air. I yank Seppie down to duck out of the way.

She gives me big, horrified eyes and ignores my question. "We need to get out of here."

"Who is he, though? What does he want?"

And then Wharff is soaring, flying through the air, leaving Mrs. Sweet behind. He lands right next to us. Seppie tries to kick him, but staggers, weak and off balance. I step in front of her and she falls against the railing.

He is too close, blocking our way forward with his formidable physique. "Are you listening, Mana? I like you. I don't want to have to kill you. And I only want to have to tell you this once before we duel or agree to work together or whatever it is that we do."

"Got it."

His breath is rancid and hot and I feel it in the air between us.

I hate him.

Hate is a strong word, but it's totally appropriate.

I appraise him. He has no gun, but I doubt he needs one. He's obviously aware of his powers and knows how to use them, which puts him a few steps ahead of me. Even without his powers, he is a mass of muscles. My fighting skills are not that impressive. I'm not trained. I could never win a fight.

"What is the Enhanced?" I ask.

"You. Me. People with special enhancements." He doesn't flinch. He doesn't make any aggressive movements. He seems so casual, as if the stakes are not unfathomably high. I am so out of my league.

"Wharff. Is that really your name?' I ask.

"It is."

"Okay. Listen, I get where you're coming from. Really, I do, but this whole setting off a bomb at the diner, kidnapping my friend, having the principal try to shoot me approach is not making me trust you much. You know?"

"So, what should I have done? Just asked you for your help?" He snickers.

"Pretty much."

"And you would have trusted me?"

"I would have trusted you more than I do right now."

His lip moves, just the tiniest of bits, and I wonder if it's some sort of tell for him, if it means that he's going to attack or if it means that he has self-doubt, or if it means he is trying to control his anger or his frustration. I don't know him well enough to read him.

He hurt Seppie. Honestly, that's all I need to know.

"What did you do to Seppie?" I ask. "You obviously didn't just abduct her."

"I gave her what they gave us, a few enhancements, although not quite so radical. We don't have the expertise here, just some of the technology."

"You gave her enhancements?" I almost vomit.

"She's a lucky girl," Mrs. Sweet yells.

"Yes. If they take." Wharff doesn't acknowledge that Mrs. Sweet spoke.

"You played god with her? With *Seppie*?"

"Technically I played alien. Pretty much the same thing."

I want to smash his brain in. I want to scream with rage. But even more than that, I want to hug Seppie and try to comfort her somehow, but there's no time.

"Seppie was fine and brilliant and perfect just the way she was," I sputter. "You don't have the right. Nobody has the right to change another person. What even are you? *Who* are you?"

"I am a man, an Enhanced, who escaped from aliens, who ran and learned and recruited. I am a man who is going to save this world from their threat by whatever means possible." He is angry now. It is obvious in the clenching and unclenching of his hands.

I don't care. I just want information. I just want Seppie safe. And I have to stay calm to do that, to push my anger down and ask the right questions. That's what China always does. I can do that, too. "What's the big deal about the crystal?"

"The crystal will arm a weapon that will kill all life encoded with a certain variant of DNA." He cocks his head to the side as if he's listening to something we can't hear.

"The genocide machine?" Seppie asks and I know she's just asking to keep him talking. The longer we can keep him talking, the better.

"Pretty much. The DNA can be alien or human, but it has to be installed into the crystal and then activated by two of the Enhanced.

Originally, it was created to kill off all humans, but the chip that was meant to activate it was harmed. That was the chip your mother had. The Enhanced were scattered throughout the world, waiting for the machine's activation, some unknowing, some knowing. I have killed most of them."

"You killed them?" I think about that sweet-looking Australian guy, the panic in his voice the last time I saw him through the crystal.

"They couldn't be controlled." He cocks an eyebrow as if saying I should make sure I can be controlled or I'll have the same fate. I get the message.

Seppie's hand touches my arm, but I don't trust Wharff enough to turn away and look at her to see what she wants.

"So you want to use the crystal to kill off the aliens? Even the good ones?" I ask.

"They don't belong here," Mrs. Sweet yells. "Can't you see that?"

"Why did the aliens even need a crystal? Why not some flood, or just kill everyone with lasers or something?" Seppie blurts from behind me.

"They want the planet and its ecosystems intact. Who wouldn't? It's beautiful and bountiful, this Earth. Part of the heightened response and urgency is because humans are having such a horrible impact on the environment. We're a nuisance. A nuisance that is hurting that ecosystem with bombs and pollution, radiation." Wharff's lip twitches as he talks.

"If they are so advanced, can't they just fix that?" Seppie asks.

"Maybe. I don't know. I imagine it's a lot of work compared to this."

"And they haven't used the crystal yet because?" I ask.

"They were biding their time, hoping the humans would straighten themselves out. We are failing their expectations. And it was stolen from them recently, thankfully."

"Well, maybe a nice chat would have been a good idea. Why does nobody just talk things through?" I blurt.

"We are."

"After you kidnapped me," Seppie says.

"And you killed that waitress," I add.

"She was annoying. And I didn't mean to. It just happened. It's no great loss."

And that is it. That is when I realize that no matter how much benefit of the doubt I would want to give him, this guy does not care about individual people. He has no remorse about Seppie, about the waitress (who *was* annoying). He just wants to have his ends achieved. He is a psychopath or a sociopath. I can never remember the difference, but he is definitely one of them.

"Can't we just destroy the crystal?" I ask.

"It is indestructible."

"Indestructible," I repeat.

"It means it can't be destroyed."

I swear people think I'm an idiot. I ignore this and say, "So, everyone wants it. China's bosses want it to destroy the aliens. You want it to destroy the aliens. The original aliens—"

"The Nephils, also known as the Nephilim, or the Nihilim, or the Nefs—you can spell that last one with a *ph* instead of an *f*," he interjects in a show-off way.

"They want it to destroy the humans so that they can have the planet intact and free to use."

"Actually it isn't the Nephils who want it. It is the Samyaza. You met one of them. Dakota Dunphy," he corrects me.

"Wow," Seppie whispers. "You're bleeding a lot, Mana."

"Why does everything always have to be about destruction?" I yell, ignoring her, and my body pumps full of rage and adrenaline at how incredibly horrible our species can be. "Why can't everyone just work things through?"

I am a dog with bared teeth. I am a tsunami wave heading toward a shore. I am anger bundled up and focused.

"Mana . . ." Seppie's voice is behind me, a prayer and a warning.

And then something hits my leg and the world fades into darkness, followed by bright, horrible, burning light and I lash out, blindly. The crystal is in my pocket. I can't let him find it. I can't let him use it. I can't.

I've fallen and hit my head, and I'm not sure why. I just know that Enoch, my sweet dog, is twenty times her normal size, and she's in front of me growling and barking. Wharff fires at her and I scream but the bullets just bounce off her furry chest. One rebounds back into Wharff's leg and he screams in pain. He jumps down onto the grass. One leap more and he's out of our sight lines.

"Holy. . . ." Seppie swears up a mother lode of curses that probably could enter the *Guinness World Records* and ends with her yanking me backward with her. "What is that. . . . ? What is that thing?"

Enoch turns and stands above us, large and drooling, a monster of a dog. Her teeth are easily as long as my forearm.

"Enoch?" my voice whispers. "You okay, baby? Good dog . . . Good dog . . ."

"Is that the dog you saw outside of world history?" Seppie is still pulling me backward, but I brace myself. My head pounds. It's hard to orient myself.

"Yes." I reach my hand up and out to Enoch. She sniffs it and licks it and starts trying to wag her tail. Her tail wallops the side of the building and creates a breeze. "Thank you, honey. Is he gone? Should I go catch him?"

Enoch cocks her head and leaps off the catwalk, rushing down and out of the building. I spring to life after her and mutter, "Crap," because I'm not up to leaping and running and springing.

Seppie is by my side, instantly. "She'll be okay. She'll come back."

"What if she doesn't?" My heart breaks just thinking about it.

"She will. Let's get out of here and try to find Lyle and the others, okay?" she asks.

"Okay."

Seppie makes a noise that sounds like a sob caught in her throat. "I'm sorry he hit you," she says.

"What did he even hit me with?" I ask.

"Energy." She pauses. "I think."

I would nod, but my head hurts and my arm hurts and I just want to get out of the bunker and find the Futures and make sure everyone is okay, to get Seppie to the hospital and checked out, and maybe to call China. But first things first. I have to get us out of here.

CHAPTER 16

We limp out of the building. There are people tied up and restrained by the Futures. Gunfire continues to the right. There is a dead woman *and* a dead student, Caleb. I think his name was Caleb. My heart feels like it might explode in sorrow. Above us, something zooms into action, loud and fierce. A helicopter, but not like any I have seen before. It's sleek and dark with no symbols on the sides. It blots out the sky for a moment and heads away.

"Crap. Is that him?" I ask Seppie as we track the helicopter southwest.

"I bet. He's a calculating bastard with a lot of resources." She spits blood out of her mouth. "I have no doubt he had an escape route."

Her blood terrifies me. "You need to get to a hospital."

"So do you."

I tap my pocket, searching for the soda bottle, which would make me feel better, I think, and then realize it—something is missing. Not the soda, but the crystal.

"Holy . . ."

"What?"

I don't even know how to explain. "The crystal. He took the crystal. He must have pickpocketed it or something when I fell."

"You had it on you? You didn't fall. He hit you with some kind of blue light thing. It came out of his mouth. It was nasty. It smelled like scotch mixed with spaghetti sauce."

"Crap." I am panicked. Absolutely panicked. "We have to stop him."

"He is *in* a helicopter."

I shake my head. "There's got to be a way. Some way . . ."

Just then, the trainees march our principal out of the bunker. She's bloody but alive. Her hair is no longer a perfect helmet befitting a senator, but a bedraggled mess. I launch toward her, grab her by the shoulders in an angry Shatner move, and demand, "Is there another helicopter?"

She laughs. "Like you could fly it."

This is truth. But it means there is one.

Janeice bangs forward. "I can fly it. I've been taking lessons for forever. Where is it?"

Principal Sweet does not answer. I resist the urge to kill her.

Seppie points. "The other one came from the roof. There's a secret roof beneath the earth. It retracts. The ground retracts, I mean, to reveal it. When it's closed it just looks like woods. There are helicopter landing pads up there."

Blood drips out of her mouth again. I point at Abony. "Get Seppie to the hospital. Please."

Abony marches right over and grabs Seppie, who is too weak to protest much.

As she half drags Seppie away, I gulp down some soda. Power courses through me. I grab Janeice by the waist and say, "Well, let's hope you can fly this one. Anyone know about Lyle?"

"He's fine. He *was* fine—" Janeice's sentence dissolves into screams as I tighten my hold on her waist and leap up about six stories to land on what is clearly a helicopter pad, which is amazing both because I guessed accurately where it would be and because it is so fancy. Everything about this place is stunning—how it remained hidden for so long, despite it being so big. How it uses the natural environment to mask its true nature. I'm glad Wharff didn't take the time to retract the roof and hide the pad again.

"*Warn me next time*," she demands as we stare at the helicopter, which is black and sleek and military-style all at once.

"Are those guns under there?" I ask. Power buzzes through me. It feels good, almost too good.

"Get in before we lose him, but yes." She jumps into the pilot seat and immediately starts flicking switches. "Okay . . . Okay . . . Hold on . . . Let me figure all this out . . . It's not the same as the one I've been . . . Okay . . . Yep . . . This features a coaxial rotor design with counter-rotating ridge blades."

"English?"

"It is a sweet, sweet machine that lets us go vertical and forward, and in the back is a kick-butt pusher propeller for high speeds and it is so pretty, such a clean sheet design. Buckle up."

I have no idea how to buckle up and by the time I have figured it out we are already lifting up and away. Someone shoots at us, but it just pings off the sides of the helicopter. Who did that? One of Wharff's cronies, I guess. The fake ground begins to retract over the landing pad, but we easily clear it.

"I see him," she says, pointing. I can barely hear her. She grabs headphones and so do I. There's a switch I have to turn on but then it's just like telepathy. "He's up there. Holy—What's that? At your six?"

"The government," I say as I make out what I assume is the Northeast Saucer. I shudder thinking of the whole event at the diner. "They are coming to wipe everyone's memory. Do they teach you guys to hold your breath?"

"Yes. But you can only hold it for so long, you know. Nothing we can do about it now. Let's catch up to this scumbag."

"How do you know he's a scumbag?" I say as the saucer hovers over the spot where we just were. Gas bellows out of the bottom of it.

"Kidnappers always are." She says this so matter-of-factly that despite all the adrenaline and craziness, I actually envy her. She believes in polarities, in black and white. There are no moral grays in the world of Janeice. I'm just glad she's on my side. Then I have a thought. "Wait. How did the government know to come? At the diner they came because of the bomb Wharff set off. The Men in Black came because of the tracking device on the bus. I guess it's all more connected than I realized."

Wharff met China at the diner because China's agency was looking for information about the crystal, but Wharff was really there to meet me because he suspected I had it. He blew up the diner because he wasn't getting anywhere. I still didn't go with him and stayed with China. Then the U.S. government sent the saucer to cover it up. Now, the government is covering up Wharff's actions again. That seems pretty connected. No wonder he has so many resources.

"Is that guy Wharff?" She gestures toward the copter in front of us.

"Yeah."

"Maybe he told them. Maybe he's on the government's side, or they are on his."

"Do not make my head explode."

"Naw. That would be messy."

I can't tell if she's kidding or not.

Out of nowhere she goes, "Hold on. I want to try this button out."

"Hold on to what?"

She doesn't answer, just presses the button and the helicopter shudders. The screen in front of me reads *Missiles Armed*.

"Do we want this guy dead or alive?"

"Well, I would rather not kill anyone. I mean, I didn't even kill my principal, Mrs. Sweet, and she's a super-jerk."

"Your kindness will haunt you someday, I freaking swear." She scoffs. The screen flashes the words *Ready Now*. I try to back away, but I have nowhere to back away to, honestly. "Is that a touch screen?"

"I think so." She reaches over.

Slapping her hand away, I yell, "Don't touch it!"

The helicopter in front of us flies over a mountain. The Google map I studied said it was Cadillac Mountain, which has a road that's not open to motor vehicles in the winter, but there's a parking lot and visitor center on top. Wharff's copter circles back around.

"Is he landing?"

"I think so," she says. "Us, too? Or you just want to zap him with a missile?"

"It's sort of a tough choice, honestly."

"I vote zap."

"He hasn't zapped us."

"He hasn't zapped us because he needs you. It's obvious. Duh."

Sometimes I do not like Janeice. Wharff's helicopter whips around so I can see who is inside, and it's him and one other guy—one other long, lanky guy with ridiculous eyebrows.

"Oh god . . ." I mutter.

"Lyle got freaking captured!" Janeice pounds her thigh with her fist so hard I think it's a miracle she doesn't break a bone. "What an idiot."

"Is he alive?" My insides have suddenly hollowed out. Anxiety races through. Lyle. Lyle can't be dead. Not Lyle. Never Lyle.

"I don't know. If he is, I will kill him," Janeice growls. Her anger is contagious, and all the anxiety inside of me splinters into a thousand parts. Anger doesn't begin to explain it. Sorrow doesn't begin to explain it. I am a mountain of fury, a fire moving through dry trees during a windstorm. I am screaming for her to land the helicopter even as Wharff's copter lands, facing us. He's out first, yanking Lyle out with him and dropping his limp body on the ground. I've unbuckled before we land and Janeice is screaming for me to wait, but I don't wait. I open the door while she's still about twelve feet up and I land, hard but well, and I use that momentum to fast flip forward, kicking at Wharff's face as I enter his space. I make contact and he *oomphs* backward. I get the first hit and it's a good one.

I know I can't win this fight.

I don't care.

My fists have lives of their own, but they aren't as strong as my elbows. "What have you done to him? What did you do to him? What. You. Agh."

One strike. Another.

My words don't make sense. Even I know that.

Wharff's do, though, and he roars, pushing me full force away. "Get off me!"

I fly through the air and land against Wharff's helicopter.

He stands, but he's obviously hurt from that bullet. He favors one side.

"Do you know what I can do, Mana?" he asks as I struggle back up to my feet. Pain ripples through my hips, which took most of the impact.

"Talk. A lot. Make some sort of nasty blue energy wave or light or something that comes out of your mouth. Talk more. Be evil. I think that's your entire repertoire, am I right?"

He half smiles. "So funny. Always so funny. I like how you mask the fear with humor, very evolved, very human. But no. I can control minds. Do you know whose mind I am controlling right now? Lyle's. I could wake him up and make him kill you. Tell me why I shouldn't?"

"Because you'd rather get the satisfaction of doing it yourself?"

"*Buzz.* Wrong answer. Because I still need you. I mean, I could find another Enhanced but the only ones I know of are in Australia, the Czech Republic, Ghana, Urzbekistan. It's all so far."

"None in South or Central America? That seems wrong. How about the rest of Asia?"

"I'm sure we are everywhere, the guinea pigs, the broken, but I only know of those that are still left. And it would take time to get to them. I am sick of waiting. I want this done now, you and me, on top of a mountain. It seems fitting. Did you know that this is where Americans can first see the sunrise every morning? Unfortunately, I don't want to wait until sunrise. Do you?"

"Are you actually asking me what I want?"

"Yes."

"I would like for you to give me the crystal, for the crystal to disintegrate, for everyone to be nice and kind, for the bad aliens to leave us alone, for us to leave the good aliens alone. World peace. A clean environment. An end to racism, sexism, human trafficking, and pretty much any form of bigotry. I'd like to feel smart and loved and have my mom wake up and for everyone to be safe."

He starts laughing. Real laughing. The kind of laughing that involves bending over at the waist. Finally, after a good twenty seconds of this, he stands up again totally straight-faced, like he never laughed at all, and he says disdainfully, "You are such a child."

"She's a dreamer. That's not childish. It's hopeful." Janeice has come out of the helicopter and she's got a gun trained on Wharff. Her hand doesn't even shake.

He laughs at her. "The wall speaks."

He snaps his fingers. She crumples to the snowy ground, the gun still in her hand, unused. She does not move.

"It's too bad you don't have mind control as an enhancement. You should have seen them all follow me at the hospital, when they were trying to kidnap you. Oh . . . It's fun," he says to me, turning his back to her. "Maybe you could have all your wishes then. People could be kind to each other, stop the war and hate. If you got good enough at it, you could make the world so kind."

"Like you care about that."

"I care very much about that! That's why I'm doing this. I'm trying to fix things, give our world time so that we can save ourselves."

What do you say to someone like this? Someone who rationalizes genocide? I'm not sure you can say anything.

He jumps and I jump at the same time, somehow sensing his attack. We meet in the air.

"I can have her kill you and she will," he whispers in my ear as he locks his arm around my neck. "It would be so easy."

"You could kill me in the headlock right now, so you obviously don't want me dead."

"Not yet."

"Exactly."

We hit the ground, a twirling mess of limbs. The snow seeps into my pants, stings my face as he sticks my head into it. I try to buck him off. I can't. He yanks me to my feet, arms behind my back. Seppie did not teach me the Krav move for this, but I have my own special skills: I spring into a back twist. The momentum of my jump yanks my arms free and my torso connects with his face as my body attempts to ascend. It ruins the move, that hit, but it doesn't matter, I was ready for it, and now I'm free. I launch into another tumbling run because it's faster for me than scrambling and my movements are harder to predict. I land by Lyle and try to yank him up so I can escape with him, but Wharff still has the crystal. The world, the aliens, or whoever gets final use of it . . . It's so confusing, but I know I have to keep it safe and keep it from him. I let Lyle go and rush back toward Wharff.

"Janeice!" he barks. "Train the gun on the boy."

She stands up and moves forward, all the way forward to Lyle, and puts the gun at his temple. His eyes are still closed.

I gasp and fight harder, but Wharff blocks every hit that I try to make and I fall, trying to fight against him from the ground where I am at a massive disadvantage.

"Janeice, kill him if she keeps fighting."

I stop fighting. I don't know what else to do. I just stop. I was losing anyway.

Wharff stands there as the wind blows snowflakes around us. I am still sitting.

"We're in a mini–snow globe," he says. "How sweet."

If I was the type of person who spits, I would spit right here. Instead, I ask a question, stall. "So, you were the person who brainwashed everyone at the hospital?"

"I was trying to get them to kidnap you." He shakes his head, casual again despite his ruffled clothes and wound. He sticks his tongue out and catches a snowflake on it. "Honestly, Mana, you are always one step behind, aren't you?"

"Pretty much," I admit.

"To be fair you have a lot of catching up to do." He sighs. "I understand that. So, I'm going to give you a brief summary before you help me save the world from the disgusting parasites that mutilated us, that are waiting to kill us. You ready?"

"Do we have to do this now?" I ask. "It's cold. I'm bleeding. I'd rather beat you up."

"Don't pretend like you're aggressive. You are no beast. No bad-ass. You're a cheerleader, aren't you? You're a good kid. I saw you after the diner, trying to rescue those children, mourning the waitress despite her tedious flirting. I know who you are, Mana Trent. Let me tell you, all your life you've done the right thing, cheered other people on, made them happy. Now you're going to do the ultimate cheerleading; it's just for the human race. You should probably try to think about it that way."

"Killing does not equal cheerleading." I think there should be a better comeback here, a better way to argue, but my brain is hyper-focused on how to get the crystal without actually killing anyone, especially Lyle and Janeice. My body is throbbing in pain. I am no good for funny sarcasm.

"What you lack, Mana, is a mission. Stay with me. Stay with me . . . I've been thinking about this." He pulls the crystal out of his pocket, holds it in his hand. I want to lunge for it and grab it, but even if I got it, what then? Lyle is still knocked out. Janeice is brainwashed. I can't destroy the damn thing.

He sighs. "Are you focusing on me? Or are you just paying attention to the crystal?"

"To be fair, you talk a lot. It's easy to zone out."

"Rude."

"I know." I apologize out of habit. "Sorry."

"Apology accepted. What I was saying is what you lack is an objective, something that you want more than anything in the world. For me, it is this. The eradication of the aliens. But for you, it isn't so simple, is it? You want your friends safe, your mom back, maybe to be loved and respected. You want to have a purpose, but you are always questioning your motives, everyone's motives. You don't just give in to your higher calling—"

"Which is to be a genocidal maniac?"

"Which is to be the savior of humanity." He holds the crystal above his head, savoring it, I guess. "Purpose. It is inside all of us. It waits there, hoping to be released, to have its wings unfettered, to launch forward and roar. It talks to you, an inner voice, it whispers in your dreams, screams in your passions. It controls us. And yet you refuse to obey it."

"I don't understand."

"Humans, us, most of us are like you. We blunder around ignoring our purpose. And we never unite. It's all *live in the moment, seize the day before you die,* but the actual death part? Everyone pretends that it isn't going to happen to them. We all repress our one unifying feature. We kill each other. We torment each other. This is our purpose, to unite against an alien threat, to make the Earth great again."

Wharff is evil. I know that. But this . . . what he's saying? It reminds me of . . . me.

"I kind of feel like you're talking in circles," I say, shivering, "and it's cold, so why don't we just come to the conclusion that I am not going to help you. I am just not. There are good aliens out there, too, aliens like Lyle and Pierce and probably more that I just don't know about."

. . . like the girl in the bathroom.

"Honestly, Mana, what other choice do you have than to help me? You don't want your friend's death to be for nothing."

I blanch. "What do you mean, my friend's death?"

He motions toward Lyle. "We have to kill him, put his DNA in the crystal. The crystal needs it. It uses it to find all the other aliens. It's pretty impressive. It locates the DNA and then explodes it. All the aliens on Earth, gone." He snaps the fingers of his free hand. "Just like that."

"You don't have to kill him. You can just have him spit or bleed or pull out a piece of his hair. How stupid are you? DNA is in everything."

"He will die anyway once we enable the crystal."

This is actually logical. I wish China were here. I wish Seppie could help me out-logic Wharff. But I'm on my own.

"Still a no," I say. "Plus, he's just one alien species. We'd just be killing his species, wouldn't we? Not all of them?"

"Do you understand anything? Do you have any idea what they are planning? If we don't stop them? Stop them now? They have plans." He scoffs. "First, the biggest plan was the crystal—the ultimate device to just kill all humans. But they didn't want to have to resort to that. So instead, they worked on the Enhanced. Each of us has a chip inside of us. When that chip turns on, we become soldiers, mind-controlled soldiers meant to take down humans."

"Are there enough of us to do that? It's not like you can even find enough of us to activate the crystal."

"No. That's why they've influenced the government to make chips in our credit cards. Those will render anyone within a five-foot radius motionless. And they are creating other Enhanced constantly. The abductions are increasing and then we, the Enhanced, will turn on humans, fight with the aliens against our own people. Do you want that, Mana?"

"There's no chip in me."

"Your mother and the agency took it out. You're a lucky one. Your DNA is enhanced but the chip is gone."

"How do you know this is true?"

He doesn't answer, just moves closer to me and I let him because it means I'm closer to the crystal. I sneak a glance at Janeice. She's still got the gun to Lyle's head, but her arm is shaking, probably from muscle fatigue from being in one position for so long. Poor thing. She'll hate herself when this is over.

"Mana, you have no choice and this has gone on long enough. Even I can't keep monologuing forever."

"Could have fooled me." I smile.

He smiles back. It is not a happy smile. It is a predatory smile. "Janeice, kill him."

"No!" I'm screaming and turning even as the gun goes off, but the bullet doesn't hit Lyle. The gun isn't facing Lyle. It's facing us, me and Wharff, and I don't have enough time to react, to try to stop the bullet before it slams into its target.

Lyle jumps up into standing position as Wharff falls, backward and sideways, into the snow. The crystal rolls out of his hand and glows, burning the snow around it even as his blood seeps toward it.

"Janeice!" I yell her name, but I'm not sure why. I'm not sure what's just happened. I turn my back on her and scramble toward Wharff, who is flat on the snow. His eyes are motionless. His chest is motionless. He is vacant. Even the blood is abandoning him. It drenches the crystal, which seems to soak it in. "You poor stupid man."

I reach for the crystal and Janeice is yelling for me to stop, so I do, since she has a gun.

She and Lyle stand next to me. I didn't even see them move. "You can't touch it. It has that guy's DNA in it—Enhanced DNA. His blood touched it. If you touch it, you might activate it."

"I thought it needed two Enhanced to activate it," I say.

"Yours plus his equals two." Janeice's voice is strong and sure. I think she's right.

Lyle's shaking his head and asking what is going on, but we don't answer him because we have to figure that out, too.

"I thought you were hypnotized or mind-controlled or whatever," I say, and I hug her. She one arm–hugs me back. The gun dangles at her side. "You saved Lyle."

"Nope. I was faking it. I'm Enhanced, too," she says, matter-of-factly. "I can't be mind-controlled."

"I didn't know that."

"Nobody does," she answers. "I was abducted for years. My mom, too. I think it's different than how it happened to you, but it happened."

I stare at her blankly.

"Nobody in the agency knows. Nobody but my mom knows."

"You hid it?"

She half shrugs like the conversation isn't worthy of pursuing. "I'm slow to trust people, honestly, and once I got there it became really obvious that the people at the agency are slow to trust, too. I mean, look at how they treated you because you're Enhanced."

Janeice is tactical and smart. I let what she just said settle into my head and take a big breath. I'm so tired and woozy.

"You killed him," I finally say, looking back at Wharff's dead body.

She shrugs. "Well, somebody had to."

"Guys," Lyle says. "I'm pretty sure I was in grave, mortal danger. I'm pretty sure that I was possibly saved by one of you or both of you, and I'm pretty sure that somebody should be hugging me right now, but I'd like to know if Seppie is safe, who is going to pick up that damn crystal, who that dead guy is, and whether or not we can get off this damn mountain because it is freezing cold up here. Can we do that?"

"What do you want to do first, demanding one?" I ask.

"Hug," he admits with a smile.

I step forward and wrap my arms around him, for a second leaning into him and letting him take my weight, but only for a second because I unwrap one arm and yank Janeice in, too. She lets me, laughing.

"You all are too lovey-dovey for me," she mutters.

"Well, you're just going to have to get used to it," I say and kiss her cheek. "Because that's how it's going to be."

CHAPTER 17

Given Janeice's and my status as Enhanced, we decide it would be safest for Lyle to grab the crystal for now, and he does, wrapping the edge of his shirt around it to pick it up. We even find a nice metal container inside the helicopter and put the crystal inside of it. We are super-careful that Lyle is the only one who touches it. We think that more than one Enhanced has to touch it at the same time, since I've handled it before and nothing happened, but we really don't want to make a mistake here, especially since that mistake could kill us. When Wharff bled all over that crystal, we think he triggered it to make it so it will kill all the Enhanced once two more touch it. We might be wrong, but it's too big a risk to take.

Once the crystal is contained, we wipe Janeice's prints off the gun and throw it next to Wharff before we get in the helicopter again. We buckle up and fly off the mountain.

"It seems wrong to leave him there," I say as we lift up, the helicopter's rotor blades cutting through the air, shooting more snow onto his lifeless body.

"The government will come get him. They always do." Janeice says this as if it's not a big deal at all, and I guess for her, it isn't. She's far calmer than I am and she knows more. I'm guessing that she knows a *lot* more. Via use of the technological marvel that is the cell phone, we contact the other Futures and decide to land on the ball field by the YMCA, which is, I guess, where Life Flight helicopters land for medical emergencies.

Lyle hangs up the phone after this is determined.

"We probably should take you to the hospital," he says.

"I'm fine."

"You're bleeding. You have a gun shot wound. Seppie will have to go, too." He shakes his head.

"I think the others were already taking her," I say.

"I hope she remembered to hold her breath when the gas came. I hope they all did," Janeice says as she lands the helicopter on the field, which is literally about two minutes away from the top of Cadillac Mountain. "It would suck to have to explain everything that happened to everyone."

As we're getting out, a Jeep barrels up and slams to a stop on the snow, just a couple yards away from the helicopter's whirling blades, which Janeice shuts off. She taps the control panel goodbye and tells it she's going to miss it, but my attention isn't on her. It's on the Jeep, and the large man hauling ass out of it and toward us.

"China!" I've already opened the helicopter door and I'm running across the couple of feet and launching into his arms. He wraps those same arms right around me, laughing.

China engulfs me in a massive leather-smelling hug. "Kid, I am so pissed off at you, but thank God . . . thank God, you're okay. I'm so mad at you but so relieved. Tell me everything." He swings me around in the air and then releases me, but keeps his hand on my elbow like he's afraid I might take off. "You trust me again?"

I do trust him again. I think of him as this all-knowing authority figure, but he isn't. Sometimes he's just as powerless, just as much a pawn, as I am. And I bet he hates it, too. I tease, "Lyle said you were okay."

"The world has obviously ended." He laughs.

As quickly as possible, I let him in on everything that has happened. Lyle and Janeice join us and occasionally add a detail or two.

And I finally tell him about the crystal.

"The only way to ensure your protection is to keep that with an Enhanced, since that's what it's been charged with, and unlike regular humans or aliens, you'll die if it goes off," China says. "You all aren't going to want to kill yourself. If it had been charged with a human, they'd be the ones who died. If it had been charged with Lyle, it would have been the aliens."

"And you suddenly know all about the crystal how?" I ask. I try to put my hands on my hips, but everything hurts too much and I sway, losing balance.

China, Lyle, and Janeice all lunge to catch me before I hit the ground, but it's China who picks me up in a sweeping gesture that reminds me of knights and firefighters and also like a basket catch in cheering. Seppie is good at that catch. She really excels at everything.

My voice cracks out, "Seppie?"

"Already at the hospital," China says. "Which is where you will be soon."

His face fades in and out.

"I can carry her," Lyle says.

"Sorry, bud. This time I've got her." China tucks me into the backseat of a car. "You guys meet us at the hospital, okay? Janeice, take the crystal."

She starts to protest, but China shuts the car door and I can't hear any more. A minute later he's in the driver's seat.

"I'm pretty mad at you," I croak.

"I'm pretty mad at you back," he says, "but I'm thankful you're alive."

We are silent. The car moves forward and turns. My head lurches.

"You didn't tell me about the crystal," he says, "and you ran away from the compound."

"They were going to kill me."

"No, they weren't. That was just Jon being Wharff's mind-controlled pawn. Nobody was going to kill you."

"Well, you didn't tell me stuff," I protest.

"True."

"It's hard to trust people when they don't tell you everything."

"Which is why you did it, too?"

He has a point. I sigh. "Even?"

"Hardly." He stops the car. "We're here."

"Already?"

"Already." He's out of the car and opening the door, assisting me so I don't fall down onto the snow-covered pavement.

I let him help me and try not to wuss out about how much everything hurts. I'm a cheerleader. I'm used to falling and being banged up. I'm not so used to being grazed by bullets and thrown around on the top of mountains, but I feel like I should be tougher somehow.

Enoch comes thundering down the road, sprinting. Her dog fur flows from the force of the run and the wind, snowflakes stuck to it. I've never seen such a beautiful dog. Ever. My heart soars. "Baby!"

She slows down so that she doesn't knock me over, and licks my cheek, nuzzling my hair with the bottom of her chin like she's claiming me.

"That dog loves you."

"I love her so much."

"I'm pretty sure she's not a dog."

I sway. "Me, too."

China insists on carrying me again and I let him, as Enoch trails behind us, and I say, "I feel like we don't have closure. Like we need to talk more."

He laughs. "The only real closure is death, Mana, and I don't think we're ready for that yet, right?"

"Right," I say. "Right . . ."

But I can't bring myself to laugh about it the way he does. I can only close my eyes and let the world fade away.

It turns out that I have a concussion and the hospital, which is so small and adorable, wants to keep me overnight. Janeice and China take turns guarding my room. Seppie is in here with me and she's staying overnight, too, and getting blood transfusions, but none of us is sure why. Enoch sneaks in and hides in the bathroom whenever any attendants come. Seppie side-eyes her a lot, but I convince her that whatever the hell Enoch is, she's on our side.

"She is *not* a normal dog," Seppie says.

"No. No, she isn't. She is even better."

"You've always wanted a dog."

"Pretty much." My mom never let me have one. Maybe this was why. Maybe she knew that some dogs are a wee bit different.

The room phone rings and China answers it. His back stiffens and he talks into it softly before he hands it to me. "It's Pierce."

I pretty much snatch the phone out of his hand. "Pierce!"

"Mana."

I look up, addressing the room. "Can I have some privacy, guys?"

There is a lot of grumbling, especially from China and Lyle, and Enoch pretty much has to herd everyone out through the door, even Seppie who is currently between transfusions. The phone is heavy in my hand as I say, "Are you okay?"

"Yes. Are you?"

"I think so. I'm just . . . I'm kind of confused. At first we thought you were probably dead. Nobody heard from you at all. And then . . . Did you send the girl to the bathroom? Was that you in Australia? Is the guy okay? Wharff said he killed the Enhanced who didn't cooperate, or had them killed."

"Mana. You always have so many questions." She almost laughs.

"It's because I'm always so confused."

Now she does laugh. "I don't have a lot of time, but I'll try to answer your questions. I stole the crystal. That is a long story. I gave it to Madison. I was in Australia protecting another Enhanced. He has survived. Hopefully, you'll meet soon."

"Madison died."

"I know."

"I'm so sorry."

"It's not your fault, Mana."

It feels like it is. I plunge my hand in Enoch's fur. "She said not to trust China."

"The agency is compromised. China still works for the agency and that makes him not quite trustworthy, not because he is intentionally doing wrong, but because he could have accidentally exposed the crystal to whoever is compromising the agency."

This makes sense. "And you're okay?"

"I am . . . okay." She clears her throat. "I don't have much time to talk, however. I just thought you might be reassured by my voice and you always have questions."

"I'm annoying that way."

"Not at all. You're human that way."

"I guess . . . I'd like to know . . . Why me? Why did you trust the crystal with me, Pierce? Why didn't you keep it?"

"You are good, Mana, and kind. You are strong and you want so very much to do the right thing, not just for yourself, but for the world. I can't think of anyone else that I would trust more."

She hangs up before I can say anything else. Tears come to my eyes, not because I'm sad, but because I'm so grateful. I'm lucky, really, to have someone like Pierce say that to me. I'm lucky to get to hang with Enoch and have friends like Lyle, Seppie, China, and hopefully Janeice. Bad things have happened—horrifyingly bad things like a missing dad and a sick mom and dead people—but good has happened, too. We've saved a world that didn't even realize it needed to be saved, at least for now.

I wipe at my tears. Enoch licks my hand and makes a whimpering noise. "Can you let Lyle back in?" I ask her. "Just him?"

He strides in the room and sits on the end of the bed. Enoch stares hard at him as he says, "What's up? Are we having a relationship talk?"

"Good guess." I feel a bit nervous about this, but compared to everything else we've been through? Well, it shouldn't be that hard. "I am totally confused by our relationship status."

"Me, too."

"You are?"

He shrugs. "I don't like labels, as you know, but it's sort of hard figuring us out. I mean, we're best friends. I find you attractive."

"You do?"

"Really attractive." He smiles. My heart melts a bit. "And I really liked it when you kissed me. I always like it when you kiss me."

"Cool." I sigh. "I think you're attractive, too, and I love you. You're my best friend in the world, but you didn't tell me things and that . . . hurt."

"Seppie didn't either."

"I haven't kissed Seppie."

"We only kissed once," he says. "Once really isn't enough. Unless you count those couple other times . . ."

"We probably should try it again sometime." I say this as Enoch turns her back to us like she's expecting the kiss to happen right this second.

Apparently, Lyle's thinking the same thing as Enoch because he's leaning in, hovering over me, basically, and his eyes are starting to close. This is my best friend, the guy I just saved, the one whom I adore. I close my eyes, too, and let it happen, just to see. And it feels . . . And it feels . . .

"Wow," I whisper against his lips. "Aliens are amazing kissers."

"So are genetically modified humans," he says, shifting so he's closer to me, pulling me closer to him. I rest my back against his hands. As he holds me up, he smiles at me. And then he kisses me again and it's . . . it's a million butterflies floating around us and sunlight and ice cream and good. It's good.

"I think we definitely have something here," I say after a minute.

"Yeah," he says. "Me, too."

People come looking for me at the hospital. The government. A Man in Black. A Wendigo. None of them make it to my room. The future agents and Enoch quickly dispatch them all.

"They like it way better than camp," Lyle says when he joins the rest of us in my room the next day.

"Well, it's like they have a purpose. It's good to feel like you have a purpose."

He sits on the edge of my bed. "You don't have to save the world to have a purpose."

Seppie groans. "Ha."

"It's true," Lyle says.

"So what happens next?" I ask.

"Well, we've sort of saved the world, saved each other multiple times, and now we have a crystal in a box that will kill all of the Enhanced if two or more of you touch it," Seppie says.

"And you," Janeice says. "He did something to you."

"I'm not sure what, though," Seppie admits. "The man was strange."

I don't like to think about what happened to Seppie and I don't know much about what happened to her, but my not wanting to think about it is nothing compared to what she actually went through in the last forty-eight hours. My heart hurts for her and my insides rage at the Wharff guy. But there's no point. He's dead now. Dead and gone.

Sighing, I try to find a way to breathe again, to be calm again. Seppie is the one who deserves to rage.

"You okay?" I ask her.

"Better than you, wounded warrior." She laughs when she says it, so it isn't mean. It just is.

We talk and hang out and wait for our papers to get out of the hospital. Lyle goes and gets everyone muffins and bagels and comes back with China and we all sort of just awkwardly wait to be able to leave.

It is in the middle of a Lyle and China teasing rampage that I interrupt and ask what it all means. What does it mean that Wharff was working with the United States government? Does that mean that our government was cool with killing all the aliens? The good and the bad?

"They don't see another choice," China explains. "It's hard to see another choice. It's like what you were saying yesterday when we came to the hospital. People like closure. Closure is hard to come by."

"We got rid of the crystal, though," Lyle says. "Sort of. I mean, we have it. So, no one else can use it."

"But it doesn't end the threat. There are still aliens. There are still aliens very mad at humans." China sighs. "No offense, man. There are still humans terrified of an alien threat. We are just a tiny planet, you know? And our technology . . . Well, compared to theirs? It isn't so awesome."

"So, what you're saying is the threat never goes away?" Seppie asks, sitting up straight. She moves around and does a squat like she's testing the strength of her leg muscles.

"Pretty much. Not unless there is some sort of miracle, some sort of outcome or option that nobody is thinking of."

"There's always another option," I say, but even as I say it, the hope for peace fades away a little bit. The bloody clothes I had on yesterday are at the top of the waste bin, a harsh reminder of all the carnage and chaos that always seem right around the corner. "We can't let abductions keep happening. We can't live in fear."

Our world stops once we realize the secrets that are hidden within it. Our brains have to rush to process the understanding that we are not alone, not in this universe, and not even in our own world. Our hearts can't ignore the way that feels—the threat, the hope, and the horror.

I know we all wish we could see the future some of us should have been committed to—a future where we didn't know about aliens, didn't know we'd have to fight them; a future where some of us could have normal human lives and eat hot dogs and die of old age and have babies and be psyched about binge-watching whatever sci-fi Lyle was into binge-watching or going to the best possible wedding that you know Seppie would have, and maybe she still will. Who knows? And those nice, boring, predictable futures were close. So stunningly close.

But that's not our future anymore. It's for other people. Well, it's for other people if we can spare them the knowledge of aliens, of humanity's almost-genocide, of us, the Enhanced.

*E*veryone is getting ready to go back to New Hampshire when China pulls me aside in the lobby of the hospital. "Someone wants to talk to you."

He hands me the cell phone. It's Julia Bloomsbury, looking smug and pale. Great. We have a video chat.

"Mana." She clears her throat. "I'd like to officially ask you to become an agent with our organization."

I almost drop the phone, but I don't.

I give a half of a shrug as if it's not that big a deal. "I'll think about it."

She *half* smiles. "I thought you'd try to insist that I apologize for not trusting you earlier."

"You don't seem like the type of lady who apologizes."

"I'm not."

Behind me, China snorts.

Julia adds, "But I do apologize about Jon. He is sorry as well."

"It's okay."

And those are the words that I say again once we're all outside standing in front of the yellow school bus full of future agents. "It will be okay."

I'm not so angry anymore. Nobody can tell me that I'm not worthy. I mean, look what has happened in just the last few months. I went from overprotected flyer on our cheerleading team, Mana who always fails her written tests, to someone who has changed the world, someone who is important enough to be trusted with a crystal, someone who can rescue her friends. I feel kind of proud of that. I wish my mom could wake up and see what's happened. I think she'd be proud, too. "Of course it will," China says, pulling me into a rough hug. I wince. He apologizes and then shakes Seppie's and Janeice's and Lyle's hands goodbye. He gives Enoch a pet on the head. Then, he sniffs in like he's trying not to cry, but that can't be right. He puts sunglasses on, obscuring his eyes. They must be new. "I'm proud of you."

We haven't boarded yet to go back to the New Hampshire training camp. I'm not sure why. Maybe it's because China is driving separately. Someone's probably in the bathroom. Someone is always in the bathroom.

"You want to take her?" I ask, even as I pet Enoch's side.

"She's better staying with you, I think." He gives her another rub behind her ears. She wags her tail. Mason comes running up from out of the hospital and bounds onto the bus.

"She's alien, isn't she?"

"Yep."

"Did you know that all along?"

"I had my suspicions. I did say she wasn't an ordinary dog." The sky above us is blue and bright. The slow-moving storm front has finally completely passed. I know this. But another will come.

Janeice tugs me by the arm. "Come on. We have to get going. The bus is idling and wasting gas and emitting god knows what." She coughs. It is fake. She is obviously not one for long goodbyes.

"You will keep in touch, right?" I ask China. "Because I need you to keep in touch this time. And since I'm an agent now, you kind of have to, right?"

"I will." He adjusts his glasses, pushing them higher up on the bridge of his nose. "I'm glad that I changed the top brass's mind about you being an agent."

"I think I've changed my mind about being an agent."

He jerks back, surprised. "Really?"

"Maybe." I sigh, thinking about Pierce and her cautions. "I mean, I don't know. I'm going to camp with the others. It's just . . . I just . . . I want to keep the world safe. I'm just not sure the best way to do it."

"None of us are, Mana. We just sort of flounder ahead and hope we make the right choices and decisions."

"Are there any right choices and decisions, though? Do they exist?"

"I like to think they do."

We all would like to think they do, that there are right choices and decisions, a sure straight line to doing the perfect and good thing.

I like to imagine an Earth that is happy. She is wearing blue and green and brown, a dress speckled with flowers. That's how I picture it. The tiny people and aliens on it just sort of living happily, co-existing in a way that humans haven't even managed yet—peacefully.

In my head, the world is singing, sort of humming a perfect song of happiness. From the mountains and through the deserts and across the hills and oceans, the tundra and plains, she is singing a song for us all to take care of one another, to value her and to value life—in whatever form it comes in. In my head, I am totally an optimist, I know, but I'd like to think it could happen.

I give China another hug and follow Lyle and Janeice, Enoch and Seppie, into the bus. Agent or not, it is way more fun hanging with them for a four-hour bus ride than with China. Maybe I can figure out how the agency is being compromised if I'm embedded in the organization. I'm not sure. But if it would help Pierce, I'm all for it. As we head down the aisle of the bus, the rest of the kids start cheering, loud and strong and beautiful. It makes me blush.

In the sky above us are life forms we can't imagine. On the Earth with us are life forms that barely seem real. But the sky, the earth, they are more than that. They are places where we can find love and trust and adventure; they are expanses that we can hide in or find comfort in. It's our choice.

We will keep our Earth and each other safe. We have no other choice. We have to.

ACKNOWLEDGMENTS

Thanks to Shaun Farrar who keeps teaching me how to be brave, how to have hope, and how to adventure.

Thanks totally go out to my daughter, Emily, because every book I write, I write for her. She is a hero too big to be contained by any one story.

These books would not have existed without the guidance of Melissa Frain. She is a rock star of an editor and I am so lucky that she was there to make Mana as tough, as funny, and awesome as possible. She, Amy Stapp of Awesome (new official name), and the rest of the amazing Tor crew make it wonderful to be an author. Thank you. The people who work for the publisher don't tend to get the fan mail the way authors do, but they deserve it way more. Why? Because they put up with me and do it with such kindness and grace. And they do it just to make the best books possible. That's pretty cool.

And all my thanks to Ammi-Joan Paquette for her agenting prowess. Thanks to all my friends at Wednesday night poker, at Rotary International, the Criterion Theatre, at the Bar Harbor Kids Book Festival, and at the Bar Harbor Fire Department who have put up with so much goofiness as I infiltrate their lives.

Finally, thank you to all the awesome people who send me emails and comment on Facebook and Twitter and all the random social-network places I appear. You have no idea how much you help me believe in the goodness of people. Thank you so much for being goofy and supportive and . . . well . . . yeah . . . awesome. Let's go save the world. Together.